"How are you this morning?" Jenny asked

"Improving," Lachlan said. "A good night's sleep is the best medicine. I didn't even hear you go out last night."

"Out where?"

His gaze took in her kimono and the lace edge of her nightdress. "Out to get your things. There was no need. You could have gone home and left me to sleep off my adventure."

"But . . ." She shook her head. "I am home. This is my cabin. It was left to me by my uncle, Lou Cameron, in case you're confused as to where you are—"

"Now just a minute," he said. "This is my place, and always has been. I built this cabin with my own hands."

The room tilted crazily around Jenny and she grabbed for the nearest chair.

Valerie Parv had a busy and successful career as a journalist and advertising copywriter before she began writing for Harlequin in 1982. She is an enthusiastic member of several Australian writers' organizations. Her many interests include her husband, her cat and the Australian environment. Valerie's love of the land is a distinguishing feature in many of her books for Harlequin. She lives in New South Wales.

Books by Valerie Parv

HARLEQUIN ROMANCE

2589—THE TALL DARK STRANGER
2628—REMEMBER ME, MY LOVE
2644—THE DREAMING DUNES
2693—MAN AND WIFE
2765—ASK ME NO QUESTIONS
2778—RETURN TO FARAWAY
2788—HEARTBREAK PLAINS
2797—BOSS OF YARRAKINA
2860—THE LOVE ARTIST
2896—MAN SHY
2909—SAPPHIRE NIGHTS
2934—SNOWY RIVER MAN
2969—CENTREFOLD
3005—CROCODILE CREEK

HARLEQUIN PRESENTS

1229—MAN WITHOUT A PAST
1260—TASMANIAN DEVIL

LIGHTNING'S LADY

Valerie Parv

Harlequin Books

TORONTO • NEW YORK • LONDON
AMSTERDAM • PARIS • SYDNEY • HAMBURG
STOCKHOLM • ATHENS • TOKYO • MILAN

Original hardcover edition published in 1990
by Mills & Boon Limited

ISBN 0-373-03125-4

Harlequin Romance first edition May 1991

LIGHTNING'S LADY

CHAPTER ONE

THE man was watching her.

Becoming uncomfortably aware of his scrutiny, Jenny Dean shifted sideways on her bar stool. But instead of blocking out the sight of the man's intense gaze, she brought herself into line with his reflection in the mirror which hung behind the bar. She stirred her orange juice with the straw, giving the act all her attention. Almost in spite of herself, she found her eyes returning to the mirror.

As a single woman in an outback opal mining town where men outnumbered women three to one, she was used to attracting glances and usually ignored them. The men meant no harm. But this man was different. For one thing, he didn't look like an opal miner. His expensive-looking clothes hugged his massive frame, the polo shirt and tailored jeans barely containing the muscle bulk outlined beneath them. He also bore an air of—command—the word rippled across her brain unbidden. His bearing was almost military, yet the lines radiating around his arresting slate-blue eyes suggested years of staring across vast distances.

A smile tugged at the corners of her mouth. The only weakness she perceived in him was the way his longish toast-brown hair strayed across his eyes. He kept brushing it aside with an impatient gesture, as if his errant hair was the only thing about himself he couldn't fully control and the fact displeased him. The gesture softened what otherwise would have been an overwhelmingly masculine package, making it devastatingly appealing.

Suddenly their eyes met in the mirror. He knew she was watching him. Warmth seeped up her neck and into her cheeks. Feeling as awkward as a schoolgirl, she ducked her head so that her frothy bronze-gold hair fell around her face in a concealing curtain. But it was too late. A movement in the mirror caught her eye—he was coming over to her.

'I haven't seen you around Lightning Ridge before, have I?'

His beautifully modulated voice sent a shiver down her spine. She kept her eyes on her glass, having the oddest feeling that if she looked at him she was lost. 'I don't come into town often,' she said in a barely audible murmur. Couldn't he see that she didn't want to talk to a stranger?

If he could, he chose to ignore it. 'Then you have a claim around here?'

'Yes. Out at Four Mile Flat.' There was no harm in admitting it. Assuming he wanted to, he couldn't locate her opal mine from such a vague description. There were literally hundreds of mines dotted all over that field.

'My mine's out at the Four Mile, too. Had any luck?'

She shook her head. She wasn't about to tell him that, in only two weeks of opal gouging, and with the most basic equipment and knowledge, she had made the biggest find of her life. Wrapped in her handkerchief and nestling in the pocket of her jeans right now was a gem-quality Harlequin opal, one of the rarest and most beautiful opals of all. The moment she'd prised it from the sheltering earth, she'd known it was her passport to the future, the nest-egg she so desperately needed, especially now. She had polished it roughly herself. When professionally cut and polished, it would fetch several thousand dollars, enough to see her through the next few months when she'd be unable to work. Selling the mine itself would provide the rest of the money she needed.

The man rested his forearms on the bar and propped a boot-clad toe on the brass foot-rail. Her downcast gaze caught the ripple of muscles as he moved and something stirred inside her. Her stomach muscles cramped in unwilling response. Who was he to have such an instant and disturbing effect on her?

In defiance, she raised her eyes to his, feeling a shock like electricity arc through her. It was a shock almost of recognition, as if she knew him from somewhere, although she'd never seen him before in her life. 'Please,' she said. Her voice came out infuriatingly husky and low. 'All I came in for was a cool drink, in peace.'

'Then let me buy you one. No strings, I promise.' He offered her his hand. 'My name is Lachlan Frost.'

'Jenny Dean,' she said without thinking. She hadn't meant to tell him her name, but city politeness was too deeply ingrained. 'I can't stay. I have an appointment.'

It was true. To celebrate her spectacular find, she was on her way to see Lucy Baxter, one of the Ridge's two hairdressers. Lucy's husband was an opal miner and Lucy ran a part-time business from the front room of her cottage in Morilla Street. Jenny was looking forward to having her hair done, as a change from the heat and dust of opal mining. She checked her watch. There were still fifteen minutes to go before her appointment.

'You're not from around here, are you, Jenny?' Lachlan Frost asked. He used her first name as if they had known each other for a long time.

'What makes you ask?'

'At the Ridge, time doesn't have the same meaning as it does in the cities. Appointments are unheard of. It's one of the reasons why people come here for a holiday and stay for a lifetime.'

She sensed the question behind his words. He wanted to know if she was a one-time visitor who'd decided to stay on. Many people did. The Ridge was home to people of all ages and nationalities, all drawn to the easygoing way of life and the chance to make their fortune.

She understood their feelings. She'd been in love with Lightning Ridge since she was twelve years old, spending school holidays with her uncle at his mine. From Uncle Lou, she'd learned how to sink a shaft and gouge opals with the best of them. When she hadn't been working alongside him underground, she'd gone noodling for overlooked opals on the mullock heaps of old claims, along with the other children of Lightning Ridge. Those days had been the happiest of her life.

They had ended abruptly with her mother's death when Jenny was sixteen. The diagnosis had been leukaemia and the end had been tragically swift. It had been left to Jenny to keep house for her father and bring up her twin brothers, who were only eight when Marian Dean died. Visits to Lightning Ridge had become a luxury she couldn't afford.

Then had come the news that Uncle Lou had suffered a fatal heart attack while underground. He had been over seventy. Jenny wasn't sure of his exact age, but she knew it was the way he would have wanted to go, while searching for his dream opal. She mourned his passing but consoled herself that he had led the life he'd wanted to lead, even if she had been the only member of the family who had approved of his lifestyle.

It had come as no surprise when a mate of Uncle Lou's had forwarded a letter from him, written just before he'd died. In it, he said he wanted Jenny to inherit his opal mine. She had promised herself that, as soon as the twins were old enough to cope without her, she would revisit her mine. She had no idea then how much she would need its sanctuary when the time came.

Two fingers snapped in front of her face. She blinked. 'I'm sorry. I was daydreaming.'

'You looked as if the weight of the world were on those fragile shoulders,' he observed. 'Are you sure you won't let me buy you a drink? Another orange juice, maybe?'

'No, thank you.' Her memories had mellowed her mood and she refused him with gentle courtesy. 'I really must be going.' She drained her glass and slid off the stool. 'I'll see you around.'

In a place as small as Lightning Ridge, which boasted a population of only eight thousand people at its busiest, seeing him again was more than a possibility. She didn't know whether to be glad or sorry. Lachlan Frost disturbed her in a way she didn't care to think too much about. And yet there was something compelling about him, rock-like almost, as if he would be utterly dependable in a crisis.

She was aware of his slate-blue eyes following her speculatively as she left the hotel, and she had to fight the temptation to look back. She didn't want to encourage him, no matter how charming and urbane he seemed. She was still a lone woman out here and she didn't need the complication.

She almost laughed aloud. Oh, no, she didn't need that sort of complication at all. After the experience which had driven her back to Lightning Ridge, she wasn't about to rely on a man for anything again. She already knew where it got her. She rested her hands on either side of her waist and arched her back, relieving the slight ache she'd acquired sitting on the backless bar stool. She was on her own and she might as well get used to it.

'Have you heard from your Dad, Jenny?' Lucy asked her a short time later, as she shampooed Jenny's hair.

The sensation felt unbelievably luxurious and Jenny's eyes drifted shut. 'No. I don't really expect to.'

Leaning over her, Lucy clucked her tongue. 'After all you did for your family; I can't believe a father would let his own daughter be kicked out, even if he did want to marry again.'

'Nobody kicked me out,' Jenny protested, gagging as soap invaded her mouth. She swabbed it away with the towel around her neck. 'Leaving was my choice. Linda and I didn't get on.'

'Then she should have left.'

Jenny gave a resigned sigh. Lucy was the most loyal person she'd ever met, following her husband all over Australia from gold mine to opal field. Her marriage vows were iron-clad. She couldn't understand a situation such as the one Jenny had left behind. Lucy thought that Jenny's father owed his first loyalty to his daughter. According to Lucy, he had no business marrying a woman who didn't get along with Jenny.

Jenny saw things differently. She knew how lonely her father had been since her mother died. No daughter could take the place of a wife—nor did she want to. The responsibility for Chris and Cal had been thrust upon her and she'd shouldered it willingly, but she was thankful that her father had found Linda while Jenny was twenty-four and still young enough to make a life of her own. The fact that Linda was closer to Jenny's age than to her father's simply meant that the twins had accepted her more readily.

Jenny's father had explained to her that Linda's first marriage had failed because of a jealous stepdaughter, and Linda counted it the worst luck that her second husband also had a grown-up daughter.

Jenny never knew whether the idea had come from Linda or her father, but it had been made clear in lots of little ways that she should think about getting a place of her own. The irony of it was that Jenny had been willing to go. It was being eased out which had hurt, after her years of devotion to the family.

Tears clouded her eyes and she blinked them away, blaming them on the conditioner Lucy was massaging through her hair. Self-pity wasn't one of her failings—at least, it hadn't been until the day had come for her to leave the Dean household. Her new flat had been waiting, provided by Jenny's father in a burst of conscience. But when it had been time to say goodbye, he'd been the only one around to see her off.

'Where are the boys?' she asked, looking around the living-room as if they might be hiding somewhere. She loved Chris and Cal with a fierce passion. Surely they would want to say goodbye to her?

Her father's face reddened with embarrassment. 'Linda took them to the cinema. She thought you and I should have this time alone together.'

'Of course.' They both knew that Linda was afraid that, when it came to the crunch, the boys wouldn't want Jenny to leave. By whisking them away, she had avoided a scene which might not have gone the way she wanted. Jenny sighed. 'It's all right, Dad. I understand.'

Her father wasn't a demonstrative man, so she was astonished when he opened his arms to her and enveloped her in a quick hug, then thrust her away.

He fumbled in his pocket. 'I have something for you. A thank-you gift for all you've done.'

'But I don't want anything. You paid the bond and the starting rent on the flat. It's enough.'

'It isn't nearly enough for eight years of your life,' he said gruffly. 'Don't think I don't know what you gave up to be a mother to us all.' He waved aside her protests. 'In a way, I'm glad it's come to this so you can have a life of your own at last.'

Too overcome to respond, she accepted the envelope he thrust out to her. It contained a sizeable cheque in her name. Her father, a modestly paid council worker, must have saved for some time to accumulate such an amount.

'It was your mother's,' he explained. 'She wanted me to give it to you as a wedding present, but I think you can make better use of it now.'

She nodded, feeling a pang. Because she'd only had one boyfriend since leaving school, he thought she was never going to get married so she might as well have the money now. Tears prickled the backs of her eyes and she picked up her suitcase. 'Goodbye, Dad.' That was the start of her new life.

Establishing herself was harder than she'd anticipated. Her only training was a correspondence course in interior design, chosen to allow her to work from home, fitting in assignments around the twins and their needs. It had worked out better than she had hoped and she'd made a name for herself as something of an expert in restoring old houses. But jobs in her field were few and far between, and her first forays yielded casual assignments but no offers of full-time employment. The money from her father kept her afloat during those difficult months.

The loneliness added to her difficulties. After years of living in the boisterous company of two young boys and their army of friends, the silence in her flat seemed deafening. If it hadn't been for Derek Sloan, she would have gone mad.

The son of a wealthy stockbroker, Derek had followed his father into the world of finance. They'd met when Jenny took the twins to visit the stock exchange, explaining its role in the nation's economy and letting them watch the activity on the floor of the exchange from the glass-walled visitors' gallery.

At first the boys had been riveted by the hectic activity, but they had soon tired of it and wandered off without Jenny's noticing. In her haste to locate them she had blundered into a tall, angular young man in a pin-striped business suit. The man had helped her find the twins then had treated them all to milkshakes in the exchange's cafeteria. His tales of the high-flown deals he masterminded had kept Chris and Cal enthralled until Jenny had realised they'd kept the young man talking for nearly an hour.

To her astonishment he had insisted on seeing her again, without the twins this time, and had taken her out for the most romantic candle-light dinner of her life.

She couldn't understand what Derek Sloan saw in her. He was well off, sure of his future and undeniably good-looking.

'You sell yourself short,' he demurred when she raised the question in her candid way. 'From my side of the table, I see a fragile creature who bewitches me with her huge green eyes.'

'No freckles?' she asked, half teasingly. She knew only too well that her fair skin was studded with freckles after an hour in the sun.

'No freckles, sun-kisses,' he insisted. 'Besides, the same sun turns that glorious hair of yours to spun gold before my very eyes.'

It was amazing how they could look into the same mirror and see different things, she marvelled. What he saw as a glorious mass of bronze-gold hair, she saw as a tangle of waves which defied her efforts to tame it. Her freckles had been her despair for years—she had never thought of them as sun-kisses before. She smiled fondly at Derek. 'For a money-man, you have the soul of a poet,' she told him.

He might have had a poetic soul but he was morally bankrupt, she found out much later, when they'd been seeing each other for some months. As soon as he knew that she had left home, Derek turned on the charm in earnest. If she hadn't been so lonely, she would never have succumbed to it. As it was, without her family and the friends which a normal teenage time would have provided, she clung to Derek as to a life-raft.

The twins' sixteenth birthday was her undoing. She posted cards to them but kept her gifts, planning to deliver them herself on the day. It never occurred to her that Linda wouldn't want her to attend the boys' birthday party.

'We aren't having any adults, just the boys' schoolfriends,' Linda explained when Jenny telephoned to enquire about the arrangements.

'Then I'll give you a hand with the catering, and stay in the background,' she agreed readily.

'There's no need. We're hiring one of those spit-roast things and having a chef to do the cooking and clearing up, so it's all in hand,' Linda assured her.

'Then there's nothing you want me to do?' Her voice barely rose above a whisper.

'Of course there is. Go out and enjoy yourself. The boys have a mother now.'

She hung up feeling useless and unwanted. Derek took one look at her stricken expression and guided her to the sofa, where he eased her down and pulled off her shoes. Then he sat beside her and pulled her head on to his shoulder. 'It's all right. Cry if you want to,' he urged.

She cried buckets, more than she had since her mother died. Derek held and caressed her, dried her tears with his hanky and massaged her heaving shoulders.

Just when his caresses changed from comforting to ardent, she wasn't sure, but suddenly his mouth was on hers, warm and demanding. So dispirited was she that his attention seemed like a balm to her battered spirit. She found herself responding, needing the comfort of his affection to prove to herself that someone still loved her.

He took her with such gentleness that her heart ached to think of it. He knew it was her first time and wanted everything to be special, he said. It was.

The tide of his lovemaking carried her along, helping her to feel whole again. He loved her. They would marry and have their own family, and everything would be all right. The problems with Linda would ease with time, and life would right itself, thanks to Derek's love.

But instead of righting itself, life went horribly awry afterwards. When she tried to broach the subject of the future, Derek changed the subject so adroitly that she couldn't be sure it was deliberate. It wasn't until much later that she found out for sure.

'You can't be, not the first time,' he said when she broke the news to him.

'I thought so, too, but we were both wrong,' she said. 'According to my doctor, I'm six weeks pregnant.'

His face lightened fractionally. 'Then it isn't too late.'

'Too late for what?' she asked innocently.

'To do something about it.'

In horror, she realised that by 'something' he meant an abortion. He wanted her to kill her baby. She was so shocked that she wasn't able to talk to him. After an hour of trying to reason with her, he walked out.

Shortly afterwards she received a call from his father, telling her that Derek had left for America to spend some time on Wall Street expanding his knowledge of the financial world. Whether Derek's father knew of her plight or not, she didn't care. If they didn't want to acknowledge her child, she didn't intend to force the issue. She knew what it

was like to have unwanted responsibility thrust upon
you. As always, she was on her own.

The idea of coming to Lightning Ridge was so
obvious that she couldn't believe it took her so long
to think of it. Here, she could recharge her bat-
teries and decide what to do next. Once the baby
came, she could sell the mine and have enough
capital to live on until she could work again. It
would be all right. It had to be.

She toyed briefly with the idea of telling her
father what had happened, but dismissed it out of
hand. He was happy with his new wife. Linda was
bound to see it as a ploy to divert her father's attention back to herself and she couldn't handle
Linda's jealousy right now. After the baby was born
she would tell them, but not yet.

'Hey, you're not asleep there, are you?'

Jenny emerged from her reverie with a jolt. 'I
was dozing off,' she admitted. With her hair in
jumbo-sized rollers and the warm air from the drier
blowing around her head, it was all too easy to lose
herself in her memories. As Lucy freed her from
the drier and began to remove the rollers, she made
an effort to stay in the present. The doctor had
warned her that woolly-headedness was a common
side-effect of pregnancy.

'Lucy, you've lived around here for a few years,
haven't you?' she asked the hairdresser.

'It feels like ten,' Lucy said gloomily, but a glint
of humour danced in her eyes. It was her cheerfulness which had attracted Jenny to her. One
Saturday morning soon after arriving at the Ridge,
Jenny had found herself sharing a table in a

crowded café with the hairdresser, who had turned out to be only three years older than Jenny herself. Her plump figure and sun-damaged complexion made her appear older. Over coffee they'd begun to talk, and had been friends ever since.

'I wonder if you know a man called Lachlan Frost,' Jenny asked her now.

Lucy gave a low whistle. 'Lachlan Frost of Orana?'

'Then you do know him. He tried to pick me up at the hotel this morning.'

'And you didn't let him? You're mad, Jenny Dean. Lachlan Frost—and there is only one—is worth a fortune. He's also a hunk.'

Jenny wrinkled her brow in confusion. 'But he told me he has a mining claim out at Four Mile Flat.'

'So he does. But it's only a hobby. He doesn't come here very often. Too busy running that umpteen-thousand-acre property of his.'

Which explained her impression that he was well off, Jenny thought. 'Where is his mine?' she asked.

Lucy shrugged. 'You'd know better than me. I never go out on the opal fields if I can help it. I leave that to Gordon.' Gordon was her husband. Lucy still hadn't forgiven him for uprooting her from a comfortable home in Albury and bringing her to Lightning Ridge.

Jenny sighed. There were so many mines scattered around the township of Lightning Ridge that it was difficult to tell who belonged to which claim. Why she should care which mine belonged to Lachlan Frost, she wasn't sure. All the same, she found herself wondering if they were neighbours. 'Has he owned the mine long?' she asked.

'You should have let him buy you a drink and asked him yourself,' Lucy teased. 'But now I think of it, he hasn't shown an interest in a woman for years.'

'Why not?' In spite of herself, Jenny was becoming more and more curious about the man.

'It has something to do with a bad marriage behind him. I don't know the details. But to answer your other question, one of his neighbours is a client and told me he's had the mine since he was a teenager. Done quite well out of it, too, she says. Enough to be able to buy Orana from his father when the old man became too ill to run it.'

A formidable man, indeed. 'I get the impression that he was a soldier. Something in his bearing,' Jenny speculated.

Lucy thought for a moment. 'Before he took over Orana, he was in some peace-keeping force in the Middle East, so I suppose he was in the army.' Lucy finished brushing out Jenny's curls, fluffed them more becomingly around her shoulders, then set the effect with a mist of spray. 'You look like a new woman,' she said, tilting a hand-mirror so Jenny could admire the style from the back.

'You're a marvel. I don't know how you got all that opal dust out,' Jenny said, reaching for her purse. If Lachlan Frost had been attracted to her as she had been, dusty and unkempt from the opal fields, what would he think of the glamorous creature in the mirror? Then she chided herself. Unless their claims were close together, she would probably never see him again. From what Lucy had told her, they were worlds apart.

She stood up. 'Thanks, Lucy. For the chat as well.'

Lucy tucked her fee into a cash box. 'You're welcome, Jenny. I get starved for female conversation, myself.' She looked at her watch. 'Look, I don't have any more bookings today. Why don't you stay for tea with Gordon and me?' She gave a conspiratorial wink. 'You can tell me more about your encounter with Lachlan Frost. For instance, do you intend to see him again?'

'It isn't likely,' Jenny said with a laugh as she followed Lucy out to the private part of the house. 'Our paths won't cross unless he falls down my opal mine.'

Later, she wondered why she had picked that particular turn of phrase. It was as if she'd sensed what was going to happen.

CHAPTER TWO

By the time Lachlan headed towards his claim at the Four Mile Flat, night was falling. He drove carefully, alert for kangaroos dashing into his path. Apart from the risk of damaging his car, he didn't relish the idea of running over an animal, although as a farmer he should have disliked the kangaroos, which destroyed his fences and grazing land.

Bracing his arms against the steering-wheel, he stretched luxuriously. Lord, he was tired. The thought of his neat self-contained cabin spurred him on. It would be good to sleep there tonight. Tomorrow he would put in a day's work underground, reminding himself that there was more to life than computers and payrolls.

Normally he would have chosen to arrive in daylight, but today he'd been waylaid by one of his father's old mates, a former opal miner who now lived in retirement in Lightning Ridge. He was a good man and he'd taught Lachlan many tricks of the mining trade when he'd first come here. Spending some time with him, listening to his stories of the old days when the Ridge had been a tiny, struggling settlement with dirt roads and no resident doctor, was little enough repayment for all he'd done for Lachlan.

Still, he felt uneasy, navigating around the opal fields in the dark, even though he knew them as

well as any man here. It was like driving around a
lunar landscape. The mullock heaps beside worked-
out mines loomed as ghostly white shapes in the
darkness. Lachlan was relieved when he spotted the
distinctive outline of his cabin up ahead.

The idea of making a cabin out of an old railway
carriage had come to him when he'd seen the
Lightning Ridge Tram-o-tel, a motel with sleeping
quarters made from old tram carriages. He'd ob-
tained the railway carriage at a government auction
and spent his spare time converting it into a comfortable cabin. With sea-grass matting on the floor
and old timber furniture from Orana, the cabin's
origins were barely recognisable. The most recent
addition was a tiny caboose he'd converted into a
bathroom.

Around him, the bald starkness of the Ridge with
its luminous white dust was pleasantly familiar. The
worked areas were fringed by stunted eucalypts and
scrub which faded into velvet darkness as soon as
he switched off the car headlights. He sighed with
satisfaction and sat for a while, letting the peace
sink into his soul.

Stretching his left arm along the back of the seat,
he was startled to find himself wishing there were
someone he could share this with. Someone like the
woman he'd spoken to at the hotel. What was her
name? Jenny Dean. The name rolled around in his
mind, as melodious as a song. She would appreciate the bizarre grandeur of the Ridge at night.

What was she doing out here? She'd said she had
a claim out this way. Was she here with her
husband? During their brief conversation Lachlan

hadn't spotted a wedding-ring, but she could have taken it off to avoid losing it. Or she could be living in a *de facto* relationship. His fists clenched. Surely she wouldn't settle for so little?

The feel of his nails biting into his palms made him relax his fingers and he frowned at what he was thinking. Why should he care whether she was married or shacked up with somebody? Didn't he have enough experience of women by now not to be fooled by a beautiful face?

Annoyed with himself, he hefted his rucksack out of the back seat, looped it over one shoulder and got out of the car. At the door of his cabin, he froze. A broom stood propped beside it. He hadn't left it there on his last visit.

Inside, there were other signs of occupancy. The fridge was in use, working off his portable generator, and it was stocked with food. Somebody had made themselves at home here.

He dropped his rucksack on the floor and checked the sleeping-alcove. The bed was made up and the sheet turned down. His unwelcome guest evidently planned to sleep here tonight. He smiled with grim satisfaction—all he had to do was wait until the man turned up. Lachlan's muscles twitched in anticipation. There would be one sore and sorry claim jumper leaving here tonight.

His acute hearing would warn him if a car approached. He decided to check on the rest of his claim. Any man who would take over his cabin so readily was bound to be stealing his opals. Picking up a torch, he let himself out again.

The signs of recent activity were everywhere. Behind the cabin he found a pile of shovels, pans, a sieve and a sharp-pointed pick. His torch also picked out a pattern of booted footprints leading from the cabin to the shafts sunk all over the claim. The intruder *had* been busy. Grimly, he walked on.

It was the most elementary mistake, and he cursed himself the second he made it. But it was too late. He felt the ground give way beneath his feet. He'd been so intent on following the footprints that he'd failed to notice the old shaft the intruder had reopened a few yards from the cabin.

The fall seemed endless, and jagged rocks tore at his skin and clothing. Then came a sickening jolt and something gave in his right ankle as his fall was broken by a support beam placed across the shaft. He hung on, hardly daring to breathe—God only knew how much deeper the shaft went. He didn't want to fall to his death.

The pain in his ankle began to radiate up his calf and he bit his lip. What a fool he'd been, walking the opal fields at night. The greenest tourist knew better than that. The whole area was pock-marked with shafts, some so old that no one knew they existed until some idiot fell down one. Like him.

His torch had rolled away as he fell and darkness engulfed him. But he wasn't afraid of the snakes which sometimes lurked in the old shafts. He'd lived on the land long enough to know they were more afraid of him than the other way around. He was more worried about passing out from the pain in his ankle, and falling the rest of the way. Would

the intruder find him in time? If he did, would he
risk his own neck to rescue Lachlan?

This thinking was getting him nowhere. He decided to fill the time by thinking about something
pleasant. Like Jenny Dean, for instance.

It was then that he heard the car coming.

Jenny hummed to herself as she drove the last few
yards to Uncle Lou's claim. Strange, but she still
thought of it as Uncle Lou's even though it belonged to her now. Navigating through the landscape at night, she was sorry she'd let Lucy talk
her into staying for dinner. She had enjoyed the
evening but the hazardous drive back made her
regret the impulse.

As her uncle's cabin loomed ahead, she heaved
a sigh of relief. Among the strange mixture of
dwellings which dotted the field, it was the most
charming and original. She switched off the engine
and lifted her groceries off the seat beside her. It
was good to be home.

The first thing she noticed was the door swinging
lazily to and fro. Her heart began to thump painfully. Burglary was rare in the opal fields but it
wasn't unknown, and there were always the
ratters—the thieves who mined claims illegally as
soon as your back was turned.

Cautiously, she opened the door and peered
inside. The cabin was empty. Thank goodness the
intruders had gone. She stowed her groceries in the
tiny galley kitchen then checked around—nothing
was missing or damaged. It was odd.

Then she heard it.

The cry for help was faint, coming from underground. Had the burglar fallen down one of the shafts? Taking a torch from the kitchen, she went outside to investigate.

The sound came again, close by. 'Help! Down here!'

Thoughts of her own safety fled from her mind. Someone was in trouble. 'Keep calling so I can locate you!' she called out.

'I'm in the old shaft behind the bathroom.'

How did he know...? Oh yes, he'd checked through the cabin first. 'I'm coming,' she called back.

'Hurry, would you? I'm not in too good shape.'

He sounded as if he was in pain. She found the shaft and shone her torch down it. 'Good grief! It's you!'

'You!' he echoed, his eyes widening with shock. 'What the hell——?'

'Never mind,' she cut across him. 'We have to get you out of there.'

'Get some help. You can't do it on your own.'

She bristled at his arrogant assumption that because she was female she was also useless. 'Where are you hurt?' she asked, ignoring his suggestion.

'My ankle. Not broken, thank goodness, but I've done some damage.'

'Can you stand on your good leg?'

'How the hell should I know? There's nothing to stand on.'

She gave a long-suffering sigh. 'What about the bottom of the shaft?'

'The bottom of the...oh, for Pete's sake!' He looked down as she shone her light into the shaft. It ended only eight feet beneath him. He could feel his face reddening as he swung himself off the beam and landed on the bottom of the shaft, taking the weight on his good leg. To her credit, Jenny Dean didn't laugh, as well as she might have done. She simply unrolled a rope ladder down to him, followed by a strand of thick rope.

'Loop the rope around your waist and I'll pull on it from here, to take some of your weight as you climb the ladder,' she instructed.

He had no choice but to co-operate. Even with Jenny taking half the strain from the top, it was a long, laborious climb. Every time he needed to use his damaged ankle, he felt like yelling aloud. Somehow, he made it to the top and untied the rope at his waist. 'Lucky for me that you came along,' he admitted grudgingly. 'I could have spent all night on that beam.'

'You would soon have worked it out,' she said generously. 'What I don't understand is how you came to fall.'

He grimaced. 'The usual way. By not looking where I was putting my feet.'

She had the grace not to say he should have known better. He was well aware of it and she must have guessed. And, in spite of everything, he was glad to see her again; her claim must be near by after all.

'Would you like to come in for some coffee?' they said in unison.

She gave him an odd look. 'Coffee sounds good, but I'll make it. You shouldn't use your ankle until you've had it checked by a doctor.'

'There's no need to fuss. It's only a sprain.'

Despite his protests, he let her take some of his weight and help him inside. With his arm lying heavily around her shoulders and her arm around his waist, they were like competitors in a three-legged race as they moved slowly back to the cabin. The beam of her torch made a jagged path for them to follow.

It was a strangely intimate arrangement. His laboured breathing sounded loud in her ears and she could feel the warmth of his body against her side. To her dismay her heart picked up speed, but she blamed it on the exertion. His physical closeness couldn't have anything to do with it.

Helping him up the few steps to the cabin claimed all her attention, then they were inside, in the orange glow of the lamps. Letting go of her, Lachlan dropped heavily on to a chair and stretched his foot out. Blood streamed from a dozen small cuts around his ankle. Quite a bit had already dried on his sock.

Jenny knelt in front of him. 'This looks bad. I'd better drive you to town to see the doctor.'

'It'll be fine once it's bathed and bandaged.' She raised hurt eyes to him, making him sorry for sounding so gruff. He massaged his eyes with one hand. 'I'm sorry, but I feel enough of a fool without going over it all again for a doctor. Everything works OK.'

'You're not just being a hero?'

'I wouldn't know how.'

Satisfied, she went to the sink and filled a plastic basin with warm water, soaked a wash-cloth in it and returned to Lachlan. When she started to remove his boot, he pried her fingers free. 'I can do it. I've caused you enough trouble for one night.'

Their eyes met and a sensation of warmth flooded through her. 'It's no trouble. I don't have anything else to do.'

'Nobody burning a candle in the window for you?'

''Fraid not.'

For some reason, this information seemed to please him. He sat back and let her minister to him. Only an indrawn breath when she removed his boot told her that he was still in pain.

She tried to be gentle as she bathed his ankle. It looked worse than it was; the cuts were minor and the main damage was a mass of bluish purple bruising around the ankle-bone.

He watched her clean and dress the cuts. 'You're good at this. Are you a nurse?'

'An interior decorator, actually,' she said, winding an elastic bandage around his ankle. 'I specialise in restoring historic buildings.'

'Interesting,' he mused. 'So where did you learn your first aid?'

'From having twin brothers who were always damaging some part of themselves.' Her eyes flickered to his face. 'You wouldn't believe the bruises Superman can get from jumping off a garage roof.'

He rolled his eyes. 'Wouldn't I? I tried it myself when I was nine.'

The trivial chatter distracted him while she finished bandaging his ankle. Nevertheless, when it was over, his face was white. 'Why don't you lie back and rest for a while?' she suggested. 'You look as if you could use a nap.'

The readiness with which he complied told her how much he needed the rest—she had a feeling that he wasn't usually a compliant man. Without a murmur, he slid down in the comfortable armchair and let his head drop against the headrest. In minutes, he was asleep.

His exhaustion probably explained why he was so careless out on the opal field. In the dark, he must have taken a wrong turn and blundered into the old shaft she'd cleaned out yesterday.

She was furious with herself for not covering the entrance. Uncle Lou had impressed on her the importance of marking the entrance to a shaft, either with mounds of dirt or a criss-crossed pattern of logs. If she hadn't been so excited about finding the Harlequin opal, she would have remembered. But the find had driven everything else from her mind.

She reached into the pocket of her jeans and fingered the gemstone. The old shaft she had chosen to work in had very little ground left unmined. Poking around in the opal-bearing layer with a screwdriver, she'd found a small but lovely nobby of opal mixed with sandstone. It had showed good colour: red, orange and green on a black backing. Satisfied with it, she had almost overlooked a second nobby nearby, which had contained even more spectacular gem colour. Rubbing it down lightly had revealed the layers of iridescent colour in a chequer-board pattern on a black backing, which made it one of the rarest of all opals. Expertly cut and polished, it would be worth a great deal.

Lachlan stirred restlessly in his chair and her attention flashed back to him. Even with his hair threaded with dust and his clothes torn and dirty from his fall, he looked so ruggedly handsome that her heart constricted in protest. In sleep, his absurdly long lashes curtained his penetrating gaze, and his mouth curved in a dreamy half-smile. It must be her pregnancy which made her feel so foolishly maternal towards him. Her fingers itched to smooth the tumble of hair out of his eyes.

He looked so different from Derek, who had slept as far away from her as possible, as if he'd disliked being touched. Lachlan sprawled so comfortably that she could imagine how his body would tangle with hers in bed. He wouldn't like his woman to be too far away, even in sleep, she thought.

Hot colour swept up her neck and face. Thinking of Derek should be enough to drive any such notions out of her head. His reaction when he'd discovered she was pregnant was enough to show her the folly of indulging in such romantic nonsense.

There was nothing more she could do for Lachlan until he awoke, so she might as well get some sleep herself. Moving quietly, she darkened the cabin and made her way to the bedroom alcove. She tiptoed back and placed a travel rug over the sleeping man, then returned to the alcove and undressed for bed.

Only minutes later, or so it seemed, she awoke to the aroma of freshly brewed coffee. It was morning and Lachlan was in the galley kitchen, filling two cups with water from the kettle. He turned and saw her sitting up. 'Coffee's ready.'

She was immediately conscious of her skimpy, lace-trimmed nightdress and self-consciously pulled the edges together over her breasts. While he attended to the coffee, she scrambled out of bed and belted her kimono-style dressing-gown around herself. 'You shouldn't wait on me,' she reproved, joining him in the other room.

'Why not? You did your share last night.'

'It was the least I could do,' she said, earning a curious look from him. He must know that it was her fault the shaft had been left unguarded. 'How is your ankle this morning?' she asked.

'Throbbing a bit and I can't put my weight on it yet, but it's improving.' He stretched languidly and his upraised arms collided with the roof of the cabin. 'A good night's sleep is the best medicine. I didn't even hear you go out last night.'

'Out where?'

His gaze took in her kimono and the lace edge of her nightdress. 'Out to get your things. There was no need. You could have gone home and left me to sleep off my adventures.'

'But . . .' She felt like Alice taking a tumble down the rabbit hole. Fleetingly she wondered if he was delirious—he must have bumped his head when he'd fallen. But his eyes were clear and his hands rock-steady as he sipped his coffee. She shook her head. 'I think you should see a doctor as soon as possible. I *am* home.'

His cup clattered back into the saucer. 'You're what?'

'This is *my* cabin. It was left to me by my uncle, Lou Cameron, in case you're confused as to where you are——'

'Now just a minute,' he cut across her, his voice as sharp as a whip-crack. 'If anyone's confused, it's you, Jenny Dean. Lou Cameron did work a claim around here, but this is my place and always has been. I built this cabin with my own hands.'

The room tilted crazily around her and she grabbed for the nearest chair. Morning sickness hadn't been much of a problem to her in the early weeks of her pregnancy, but now she felt an acrid taste in her mouth and a knot tightened in her stomach. 'What are you saying?' she whispered.

'Only the truth. You're on my claim. Was there ever any doubt?'

'Oh, yes, there was plenty of doubt.' Her voice came out in a stricken whisper. 'For the last three weeks, I've been living here thinking it was mine.'

It was his turn to stare at her open-mouthed. 'You've been here for three weeks?' She nodded dumbly. 'But how did you get in? I didn't see any signs of a break-in.'

'I've had a key for years,' she explained. 'I used to stay with Uncle Lou during my holidays.'

'Good lord! And all those years I thought Lou had a woman he wanted to impress. It was you, his niece, wasn't it?'

'I suppose so.' A leaden weight settled on her chest and it was difficult to speak. 'He let me think this place belonged to him.'

'I'm sorry, but it doesn't. Since I couldn't come up here every week, I let him have the use of the cabin whenever he liked. Having him work the mine kept my claim intact when I had to go away.' His mouth twisted into a wry grin. 'He gave me the impression he had a lady-friend staying with him, so I made myself scarce when I knew she was coming up here.'

'So that's why we never met.' She lifted pain-filled eyes to Lachlan. 'Why would Uncle Lou do such a thing? He didn't have to impress me. I loved him.'

'He was probably ashamed to let you see his old place. From what I remember, it was pretty miserable and run-down and he didn't have a lot of luck. When he did, he tended to drink. Or didn't you know?' Miserably she shook her head. 'Once he started the lie, he was probably too ashamed to admit the truth.'

'But he left me his claim when he died. It must still be here somewhere. Could you take me there?'

A frown etched his forehead. 'It won't do any good. In the first place, it was never much of a mine. In the second, it's registered to someone else by now.'

'How could it be if he left it to me?'

'The mining laws are complicated. But the fact is, a claim has to be "effectively worked" in the opinion of the mining wardens. If a mine is left untouched for too long, with no new work in evidence, an inquiry is held and the claim can be cancelled.'

'Wouldn't they contact me first? It seems so unfair.'

'Unless your uncle made arrangements to have the claim put into your name on his death, the authorities might not know who to contact. The laws were brought in to stop people staking hundreds of claims which they couldn't possibly work, keeping out those who could. When I have to go away, I get someone to work my claim or advise the mining wardens. It's a very fair system.'

Bitterness washed over her. 'It's easy for you to say. You haven't been left homeless by these wonderfully fair laws.'

He thrust a cup of coffee into her hands. 'Drink this, you'll feel better.'

The acrid aroma caught at her nostrils and she gagged. She put the cup down and stumbled to the door. 'Excuse me,' she forced out and raced for the adjoining bathroom.

Through the thin walls, he must have known she was being violently ill. But he made no comment when she returned, white-faced and trembling. 'Would you like that coffee now?' he asked.

He probably thought her reaction was due to the shock of finding out she didn't own a mine after all. She decided not to enlighten him. It served no purpose, since she would be gone by this afternoon and they would probably never meet again. 'Could I have it a lot weaker, with some milk?' she asked. 'There are some wheatmeal biscuits in the cupboard, too.'

He handed her two with her coffee. 'Eating something should settle your stomach. Then we can decide what to do.'

'There's nothing to decide,' she said dully. 'It's kind of you not to be angry at me for invading your home, but, now I know the truth, I'll return to Sydney today.'

'Then you only came here on holiday?'

'No. I intended to stay until I made up my mind what I wanted to do next,' she confessed.

He took a sip of his coffee. 'Do you have family in Sydney? Or are they the reason you're running away?'

She jerked her head up. 'I'm not running away. My father remarried recently and it was time for me to try my own wings.'

'It doesn't sound as if it was entirely your choice.'

She felt sick and miserable and the bottom had fallen out of her world. 'What does it matter?' she asked tiredly. 'I'm not your problem.'

'But I was yours last night,' he reminded her. 'I'd like to help, even if only to return the favour.'

'There would be no favour to return if I hadn't cleaned out that stupid old shaft,' she snapped back. Then her eyes widened as she remembered. The magnificent opal didn't belong to her, either. Wearily, she returned to the bedroom and retrieved it from her jeans pocket. 'This belongs to you,' she said, holding the handkerchief-wrapped bundle out to him.

He unwrapped the stone and whistled as the light caught the jewelled colours. 'Good lord, it's stunning.'

'I know. It's a genuine Harlequin. I took it out of the pillar holding up the old shaft.'

'You mean it was there all the time? I must have worked all around it without finding it.'

'It isn't unusual in the opal fields,' she agreed. 'Anyway, it's yours now.'

He heard the tears blurring her voice. 'You found it—you should keep it,' he said, holding it out.

She shook her head. 'What do you think I am? A ratter?'

'You didn't know you were working my claim, so you aren't a ratter.' He gave an explosive sigh. 'Don't sit there like Oliver Twist begging for more. I'm not an ogre and I object to being made to feel like one.'

His sharp tone eroded the last of her resistance. Tears spilled down her cheeks faster than she could wipe them away and her breath came in gulping sobs. 'I'm sorry,' she said. 'I'm not usually a cry-baby.' The assertion sounded foolish when said through a flood of tears, but they refused to be stemmed. She had never felt so miserable. The cabin which was to be her refuge until the baby came was gone. The mine which should have supported them both no longer existed. She couldn't even lay claim to the magnificent opal. It had all been a lie. What was she going to do?

Suddenly his arms came around her and she was cradled against his massive chest. It felt good to be held and comforted. 'Don't sound so tragic. We'll work something out,' he promised.

She turned tear-filled eyes to him. 'You make it sound as if it's possible.'

His hold tightened as a shudder shook her. 'Anything is possible if you believe it is. Look, why don't you stay here for a bit longer, until you decide what to do? I'll go back to Orana and let you have the place to yourself. How long do you need?'

Hysterical laughter bubbled in her throat. He thought a week or two would be enough for her to make alternative plans. 'About nine months,' she said.

His comforting arms dropped away and he limped back to the galley, where he propped himself against the breakfast bar and stared at her. 'Nine months? You mean you're pregnant?'

She dropped her head so her hair fell in a curtain around her face. 'Yes,' she said, her voice muffled. He wouldn't want her around for long now that he knew the truth.

'You don't look pregnant,' he said, sounding suspicious. Surely he didn't think she was playing on his sympathy by pretending? Her bout of morning sickness should have dispelled any such idea.

'I'm only a couple of months—it won't show for a while yet,' she explained. 'But you needn't worry. I'll go back to Sydney. Once they know what's happened, I'm sure my family will understand.'

He looked shocked. 'You mean they don't even know?'

'My father is happy for the first time since my mother died. How can I spoil things by telling him the truth?'

'How can you not? You're going to need help from somewhere.'

She shot him a scathing glance. 'I'm well aware of what I need. What I don't need is a lecture from you because I've suddenly turned into a fallen woman.'

'Stop putting words into my mouth,' he commanded. 'I don't think any such thing. I wouldn't presume to judge your character without knowing the facts. Yet you seem willing to judge mine.'

She drained her coffee-cup and stood up. 'I didn't mean to cast aspersions. I guess I'm not thinking clearly after all that's happened. I should have said I don't blame you for deciding that I'm not worth your trouble.'

His eyebrows lifted. 'Not worth my trouble? Far from it—I think it's bloody marvellous.'

She was Alice again and the rabbit hole was getting deeper all the time. 'You do?'

'Yes. If you'd sit down and stop looking as if you're about to disappear at any minute, I'll tell you why.'

CHAPTER THREE

FEELING apprehensive, Jenny sat down. There wasn't much else to do, since Lachlan wasn't about to let her leave until she had heard him out. She braced herself for a lecture.

To her surprise, he had something else in mind. 'Tell me about this work you do, restoring old properties.'

It was an odd time for a discussion about her work. 'I had to find something I could do from home, while I was looking after my father and brothers,' she began, not sure how much he wanted to know. 'I enjoyed home-making and people commented on how well I'd done decorating our home on a shoestring, so I decided to study decorating by correspondence. It seemed like an ideal career.'

'Go on,' he prompted. 'I'd really like to know about your work with historic houses.'

'I haven't done a lot,' she admitted. 'But it's fascinating, like being a detective. In order to restore the house accurately, lots of research is needed. Sometimes I have to scrape away centuries of paint and wallpaper to identify the original materials, then they're copied, usually from tiny fragments. Templates of missing plasterwork have to be made and the joinery restored to its original condition. For an old house I worked on in the Hunter Valley, I arranged for the garden to be planted with species found in the original grounds——' Enthusiasm had carried her away and she halted abruptly. 'This can't be very interesting for you.'

He arched one eyebrow. 'You'd be surprised. As it happens, I'm involved in restoring the homestead at Orana as part of the district's sesquicentenary. But I have my hands full running the property and there's still a lot of work to be done on the house. You could take it over. For wages and your keep, of course,' he added.

He was doing his best to solve her problems and she appreciated it, but she felt sure that the restoration project hadn't existed until a few minutes ago. 'You don't have to manufacture a job for me,' she said stiffly. 'I know how it feels to have unwanted responsibility thrust upon you. I wouldn't dream of imposing on you any longer.'

'I see. Do you have somewhere to go when you leave here?'

She hesitated, sensing a trap, but he could read the truth in her distressed expression. 'No. I couldn't afford to keep up my flat in Sydney so I let it go when I decided to come here.'

He nodded as if it was what he expected. 'What about the baby's father? Does he know about the child?'

Her lashes fluttered down over moist eyes. 'He knows.'

Lachlan smothered an oath. 'And he let you come out here by yourself in your condition? What sort of a bastard is he?'

'The usual selfish kind,' she said flatly. There was no point in berating Derek for being no better than he was. 'Neither of us expected me to get pregnant the one and only time we ... It wasn't what we bargained for,' she finished.

'Which is no excuse for not taking precautions or at least standing by you afterwards. Where is this excuse for a man now?'

Lachlan sounded as if he would like to get his hands on Derek, she realised with a start. Mentally, she compared the two men. Derek was as tall as Lachlan but much slighter in build. He wouldn't stand a chance against Lachlan in a fair fight. It was lucky for him that he was already safely out of the country, she thought with a faint flicker of amusement.

'He's in America,' she explained, 'so you can stop looking around for a shotgun.' It was exactly what he appeared to be doing, yet she couldn't understand why he was so angry on her behalf—they barely knew each other. Unless he was as gallant as this towards all women.

He unclenched his fists and relaxed his arms, folding them across his chest. 'How did you know what I was thinking?'

'You looked as if you could cheerfully murder Derek, but there's no need. I blame myself equally for getting myself into this. It does take two, you know.'

His speculative glance wandered over her still-trim figure. The tie-belt of her kimono had loosened and her sleekly tanned legs were bare to his inspection. It was hard to talk about making babies without bringing sex into the conversation, but she found herself wishing she had been less forthcoming. The air between them was suddenly electric.

He dispelled it by limping to a chair and sitting down heavily. 'All the same, a child should have a mother and father in evidence. It's only right.'

Pride made her temper flare. 'My child will be well looked after, with or without a father. Single-parent families are common enough nowadays.'

'Which doesn't mean they're to be recommended,' he growled.

How old-fashioned he was, even though he didn't look to be more than thirty-two or thirty three. 'Nevertheless, I wouldn't marry a man I didn't love, just to give my baby a father,' she said defiantly.

'That takes care of my next suggestion,' he said, his gaze suddenly intensifying.

She tore her eyes away. 'You can't mean you would marry me just because I'm pregnant?'

'It did cross my mind,' he said with studied casualness. 'Think about it. It would solve your problem of a home for yourself and the baby, and I'd have someone to finish the restoration of Orana.'

She could hardly believe her ears. 'Marriage isn't a solution to a problem, it's a sacred union.' At the same time, a picture of herself as Lachlan's wife flashed into her mind. He had already shown himself to be good-natured and the owner of a sense of humour—his response to his own folly last night proved the last. But marriage wasn't a job for which you could present your qualifications. And marriages of convenience had gone out with the Victorian era.

In any case, the loneliness of the last few months had convinced her that, when she did marry, it would be for love alone. She couldn't imagine a sadder existence than the one he was proposing, although she still wasn't sure whether he was serious or not.

'All right, I agree, it's a crazy idea,' he said as the silence lengthened. 'But what about my first suggestion, that you come to Orana and supervise the restoration work in time for the sesquicentenary?'

'Assuming there really is such a celebration,' she observed.

He saw what she was thinking. 'You're afraid that I made up the project to get you out of a jam. Well, I didn't. A hundred and fifty years ago this year, Orana homestead was a staging post for the Cobb and Co coaches. My great-grandfather built it and each generation has added to it, although the original sandstone building is virtually intact. I have copies of the plans drawn up by the colonial architect. The original cost of the building was three thousand five hundred pounds.'

In spite of her misgivings, she smiled. 'All right, I accept the provenance of the homestead.'

'Then why don't you come and visit it? You'll soon see whether it's a trumped-up job or not, and it isn't, I promise. Then you can give me an answer.'

The invitation was more than fair. Knowing that the opal mine didn't belong to her, she couldn't stay here for very long, so she would have to find an alternative. There was no harm in looking at Orana—she was already intrigued by Lachlan's brief description of it. Afterwards, if she decided not to stay she could still return to Sydney and her family.

The thought of her father's anguish and Linda's cool response when she broke her news to them was the final straw. 'I'll come and see the homestead, but I'm making no promises,' she said.

His look of relief was plain. 'Wonderful. We'll start back later this morning.'

'I'm afraid not.'

'Why? Is there something you have to do in Lightning Ridge?'

'Yes—get you to a doctor and have your ankle examined. There could be a hairline fracture which will only show up on an X-ray. You're in no shape to drive, so I'll take you there and back myself.' It was the least she could do after being the cause of his mishap.

His forehead creased in a frown of annoyance. 'Are you always so stubborn about getting your own way?'

'It comes from eight years of raising twin boys. I had to stand my ground or be wound around their little fingers.'

If he resented being compared with her teenage brothers, he didn't say so. Perhaps he saw the sense in her argument, because he raised his hands in mock surrender. 'Far be it from me to argue with an expert. I'll see the doctor and rest my ankle today. Satisfied?'

'Completely.'

'Thank goodness.' He looked around the cabin.
'There's only one problem. What shall we do about
the sleeping arrangements?'

In her determination to do the right thing by him,
she had forgotten that there was only one bed in
the cabin. 'I'll use a sleeping-bag on the floor,' she
decided. 'I did it often enough when I stayed here
as a child.'

'But you weren't pregnant then,' he reminded her.
'If anyone uses a sleeping-bag, it will be me.'

Her impatient sigh crackled between them. 'How
will you get into it with a damaged ankle?'

'Impasse,' he said. 'Nobody uses the sleeping-
bag.' He massaged the back of his neck. 'And I
refuse to spend any more nights in that chair. My
muscles are still complaining. Which leaves only one
alternative. The bed is big enough for two. Surely
we can share it if we're adult and sensible about
it?'

She was sorry now that she hadn't agreed to leave
right away. She could take a room in town, but that
would mean leaving Lachlan to fend for himself.
If he had another accident it would be on her conscience. At the same time, how could she share a
bed with him, however platonically? He already affected her more than she cared to admit—her pulses
picked up speed at the very thought. Except for
that one night with Derek, when she had been out
of her mind with loneliness, she'd never shared a
bed with any man.

There was also the thought of what people would
say if she shared the cabin with him. The Ridge was
a small community; gossip travelled fast and she

didn't fancy being the subject of it. But was it too late already? Had everyone but Jenny known that this was Lachlan's cabin and drawn their own conclusions? Her thoughts whirled. If only Uncle Lou had been honest with her from the start, none of this need have happened.

Dimly she remembered staying in a much more modest cabin than this one, on her earliest trips to the Ridge. With a child's candour, she had complained about the primitive conditions. Uncle Lou had been so proud when he'd shown her 'his' new cabin. Her fulsome praise must have made him all the more determined not to tell her the truth so, in a way, she was the reason for the deception as well as its victim. She sighed heavily. Poor Uncle Lou. He had only wanted to please her with what had seemed at the time like a harmless lie. It probably hadn't even occurred to him that she would assume he had left her this mine, without further checking.

However badly it had turned out it couldn't be undone, so there was no point dwelling on it. She made an effort to rouse herself. 'What would you like for breakfast?'

'I can cook it. You should be resting,' he said.

'I'm pregnant, not ill,' she reminded him. 'My doctor told me I should do whatever I like, within reason.'

'I'll bet he didn't mean opal mining.'

Her expression softened. 'Probably not, but I *was* careful. Until I found the Harlequin opal,' she added, colouring guiltily.

Grudgingly, he agreed to let her prepare breakfast while he limped off to have a shower. By the time

he returned, she was sliding a fluffy cheese ome-
lette on to his plate. He eyed it hungrily. 'It looks
good. Aren't you having any?'

She made a face. 'Toast is as much as I can face
in the mornings. I don't seem to have a problem
cooking the food, just eating it.'

'Reminds me of some shearers' cooks we've had
at Orana,' he said, grinning. 'Can't stomach their
own cooking.' He ducked as the tea-towel she
lobbed at him sailed over his head.

After breakfast it was her turn to use the
bathroom. She took her jeans and T-shirt into the
tiny caboose and dressed there, away from
Lachlan's eyes.

Emerging fully dressed, she found him outside
the cabin, propped against the wall, whittling at a
branch of dry timber. She watched curiously as he
finished shaping it then dropped it to the ground,
tucking one V-shaped end under his arm. He
hobbled a few steps to demonstrate his handiwork.
'What do you think of my crutch?'

'Quaint but practical.'

With it he was immediately more mobile. He had
no difficulty walking to her car or climbing in,
although they had a short argument over who was
going to drive. To her surprise, Jenny won.

Conscious that he was watching every move, she
drove with exaggerated care over the rough road,
slowing to negotiate the cattle-grids and gates on
their route.

'I feel so damned useless,' he growled when she
got back into the car after closing yet another gate
behind them.

'Don't worry, your turn will come once I know you haven't done any serious damage,' she assured him.

He muttered something under his breath. She didn't catch what it was but had the feeling that it wasn't complimentary.

Gradually, the lunar landscape of the opal fields gave way to the suburban neatness of the new town, where houses and blocks of land had swallowed up what some miners swore was rich black opal country. Jenny well knew that the richest opals were always in the next shaft. In this case, the truth would never be known.

The outskirts of Lightning Ridge came as a surprise to most visitors. Breasting the low ridges surrounding the area, they found themselves in an alien landscape where mullock heaps like pigmy volcanoes stretched as far as the eye could see. For hundreds of miles around the town, almost every blade of grass was covered with white dust. The only greenery was the stunted grass and shrubbery which struggled to survive around abandoned mineshafts. The road was lined with tiny wood, fibro and corrugated-iron shacks, homes to the thousands of miners who worked the area.

The town itself was in a hollow where tough eucalyptus trees and casuarinas grew wild in the sandy red soil. Jenny drove down Morilla Street, which had supplanted Opal Street as the main thoroughfare. A surprising number of shops surrounded the old Digger's Rest Hotel. Most had mining-related names like Flash Opal and Harlequin Take-away. The local newspaper was called *The Lightning Flash*. Around one shop stretched a spectacular mural two storeys high, depicting mining life.

Jenny pulled up outside the doctor's surgery in Morilla Street. 'Would you like me to come in with you?'

He shot her a look of disgust. 'I'm not one of your teenage brothers.'

As if she needed reminding! 'I thought you might appreciate some company,' she said. 'I'll get the bread and milk and meet you back here.'

By the time she had completed her errands, it was almost time to collect Lachlan. She hesitated, then went into the tourist centre to check on road conditions between here and Sydney in case the job at Orana didn't work out.

Lachlan watched her emerge from the tourist centre and his eye went to the maps clutched in her hand. 'There's nothing like optimism, is there?' he commented. He sounded put out.

She put a hand on his arm. 'What did the doctor say?'

'Exactly what I expected: there's no break and no fracture. Not even a torn ligament. I'll be back on my feet in a couple of days.'

The news was good, so why was he so moody? 'You don't sound very happy about it,' she observed.

'I can hardly jump up and down with excitement, can I?' was his gruff reply.

She opened the car doors to allow some of the hot air to escape before they got in. 'Where to now? Back to the Four Mile?'

'No. The artesian baths,' he instructed. 'Doctor's orders.'

She nodded, pleased with the suggestion. 'Why didn't we think of it? The hot mineral water is just the thing to help your ankle. I'll gladly drop you off there.'

'I wasn't planning to swim alone.'

'But I didn't bring my swim-suit.'

'Yes, you did. I threw it on to the back seat while you were in the shower.'

Doctor's orders, huh? It sounded more like Lachlan's manipulation. She bit her lip. Suddenly this didn't seem like such a good idea any more; she hadn't bargained on parading before him in a swim-suit. 'I don't think it would be good for me at the moment.'

'If you mean the baby, I asked the doctor and he said it was fine, provided the water temperature is comfortable for you.'

It was tempting. If Lucy had been her companion, she wouldn't have hesitated. Lachlan's words about the bed came back to her: 'we can share it if we're adult and sensible.' What better way to find out if she was either of those, or none of them? There was still time to book a room at the motel in town. She nodded. 'I'd like a swim.'

The pool was a short drive north-east of the town, on Pandora Street. The water which supplied it came from a bubbling mineral spring nearly four thousand feet beneath the earth. It was wise to check the temperature before plunging in—sometimes it was hot enough to burn.

Jenny hadn't visited the pool since it had been renovated for the Australian bicentennial celebrations. She was pleased with the smart new look and the safer steps which had been built leading into the pool. In spite of the warm air temperature, steam hovered above the water.

Changing into her swim-suit, she was relieved to find that her pregnancy barely showed. All the same, she was conscious of the high-cut legs and plunging back of the garment as she made her way to the pool. Lachlan was already sitting on the edge, letting his ankle swing in the hot water.

'You were quick,' she commented.

'I had my swimming-trunks on under my clothes.' He looked up; his eyes were on a level with her midriff. He said nothing, but his eyes darkened as they roved over her curves outlined in the navy maillot. 'Glad you agreed to come?' he asked after a while.

Self-consciously, she dropped down to his level. 'Yes. Although the hot mineral water makes me sleepy.'

'No problem. We can rest here for as long as you like after our dip.'

'Which reminds me,' she said, 'who's running Orana while you're out here lotus-eating?'

'An army of staff including a manager, an overseer, a dozen jackaroos, ringers, stockmen and plant operators. Orana's a big place.'

'But you still like to escape to your opal mine?'

'It's hardly an escape. Normally I put in a full working day underground. By disappearing every now and then, I keep the staff on their toes. They don't depend on me for every decision.'

'And since they don't know when you'll be back, they can't afford to slacken off,' she concluded. 'It sounds positively feudal.'

He gave an impatient sigh. 'I'm not out to trap my employees. All I ask is a fair day's work for a fair day's pay, so you can stop looking so shocked. I learned my lesson from my father, who insisted on doing everything around the place, making every decision. He prided himself on never having a day off. He had his first heart attack when he was fifty, and there was no one willing or able to take over. I don't want to be like him.'

So Lachlan's father had been the feudal one, not his son. 'Where are your parents now?' she asked.

'Dad has to take things quietly these days so they retired to the Gold Coast in Queensland, to be near my sister, Kate. She's married to a real-estate developer and they have four kids. Mum and Dad dote on their grandchildren—it's all I ever hear about in their calls and letters.'

She regarded him with surprise. He sounded as if he resented the attention his parents showered on his sister and her family. Such an image didn't fit in with what she already knew of Lachlan Frost. She remembered Lucy telling her that Lachlan had a failed marriage behind him. Maybe that had something to do with it. 'Do you have any children?' she asked.

His jaw tightened and a muscle in it worked as if he was controlling a burst of anger. Perhaps his ex-wife had custody of his children, which would explain his bitterness. But this wasn't the reason. 'No, no ties,' he said with apparent indifference.

She wasn't fooled. For some reason, he did care about not having a family. 'Don't you like children?' she asked, wondering if this explained his attitude. Unconsciously, she linked her hands across her stomach as if protecting her unborn child.

'What the hell does it matter?'

His angry outburst startled her. Before she could react, he jack-knifed off the side of the pool into the water and surfaced some distance away. Favouring his injured foot, he side-stroked further away from her.

She stared after him, her own wish to swim vanishing. What had she said to make him so angry? He might at least have told her what she'd done wrong.

When he stayed away, she stood up, gathered up her towel and went inside to get changed. The water was too hot for her to go in anyway.

She was sitting under a shady tree beside the car when he joined her outside the pool. His face was flushed from the hot water and his hair was glossy, the errant curl making an inverted question mark on his forehead. 'Why didn't you come into the water?' he demanded.

His black mood had lifted as quickly as it had come. 'I didn't feel like it,' she said stiffly.

His look was scornful. 'Surely you aren't sulking?'

She feigned astonishment. 'Me, sulking? Why should I sulk just because you bit my head off for no reason?'

His mouth tightened into a grim line. 'Sarcasm doesn't become you, Jenny. I do have the right to keep some of my private life private, you know?'

'Privacy didn't worry you when you quizzed me about my baby's father.' Anger rose in her like a tide. 'I'm just glad that it isn't you. If you fly off the handle at the slightest provocation, I can imagine what sort of father you'd make.'

The irises of his eyes darkened and a deep furrow of anger creased his forehead. 'That, my dear Miss Dean, is something you aren't likely to find out. You have as much chance of conceiving my child as you have of being caught in a tidal wave in Lightning Ridge.'

His anger whipped at her, each stinging syllable making her feel as if he were striking her physically. 'I'm glad we understand each other,' she said with all the dignity she could muster. Inwardly, she was horrified at the change which had come over him. What had happened to his good nature and sense of humour? Were they mere fronts for a hot-tempered dictator? If so, it was just as well to find out before she went to work for him. 'I'd like to go home now,' she said, then remembered that she no longer had one to go to. But Lachlan was already getting into the passenger seat of her car.

She climbed into the driver's seat and gunned the engine. The air inside the car was so hot that it hurt to breathe; winding her window down gave little relief. Beads of moisture gathered on her forehead and upper lip. She blotted her face with a tissue, her movements jerky with anger. Lachlan still hadn't told her what she'd done that was so terrible.

In a sudden burst of decision, she swung the car off Pandora Street into Opal Street, pulling up outside a motel, where she got out. Lachlan leaned across to her. 'What are you doing?'

His anger seemed to have evaporated with the short drive. 'Booking myself a room,' she said. 'I'll come back here as soon as I've dropped you back at your cabin and packed my things.'

'Why? I thought we agreed to spend the night there then drive out to Orana in the morning.'

Surely he didn't think they could go on as planned, after the scene outside the pool? 'I've changed my mind,' she informed him.

'Well, I haven't. I want you to stay.'

'And what Lachlan Frost wants, he gets, right?'

'Hardly.' He pressed his fingers against his eyes in a gesture of weariness. 'Look, this blasted foot is making me touchier than usual. I'm sorry for sounding off at you just now. Can we erase it and start again? Please?'

Charm, your name is Lachlan Frost, she told herself. The slightly crooked smile he gave her, combined with the endearing way his hair fell across his eyes, began to melt her anger. And she had thought the twins were master manipulators! They paled alongside this man.

'I shouldn't,' she said, hearing herself weakening.

'But you will.' His voice was creamy with invitation.

Indecision tugged at her. She didn't want to be at odds with him, although she avoided examining her reasons too closely. Yet he *was* hot-tempered, and she had a feeling that his anger wasn't due entirely to his injury. Should she trust herself to someone with such a short fuse? You did last night, she reminded herself.

He straightened his leg in the cramped confines of the car and groaned as he accidentally put pressure on his damaged ankle. The sound decided her. He couldn't fend for himself yet. She had no choice but to relent.

'Very well, I'll stay as planned.' As his expression brightened, she added, 'But only for tonight. After tomorrow, we'll see.'

CHAPTER FOUR

TOMORROW? There was still tonight to get through, Jenny told herself as she completed her errands in town. Lachlan's eyes followed her from the car as she crossed the street to the post office. It was almost a relief to go inside out of his view, and spend a few minutes writing postcards to send to the twins.

She had written a chatty letter to her father but hadn't got around to posting it, so she sent it with the cards. Thank goodness it had been written before Lachlan had literally dropped into her life—she had no idea how to describe him to her father. Time enough to worry about it if and when she took the job at Orana.

On her way back to the car she picked up a barbecued chicken from the take-away food bar. With some salad, it would make a tasty lunch.

'I hope you like chicken,' she said to Lachlan as she got back into the car.

'It sounds fine,' he agreed.

His voice sounded strained. She looked at him in concern. 'Are you feeling all right?'

'Perfectly. Let's get out of here.'

His snarled reply told her all she needed to know. After the doctor's probing and the swim, his ankle was painful. Risking his anger, she asked, 'Did the doctor give you some medication to take?'

59

'Some pain-killers. I had the prescription made up while you were in the tourist centre. But I don't want to take them yet—they're supposed to make you drowsy.'

'Maybe that's the idea, so you'll rest,' she suggested.

'Yes, Nurse Dean,' he said with heavy sarcasm. 'Do you think you can drive and talk at the same time?'

Gritting her teeth and reminding herself that his mood was due to his injury, not to anything she'd done, she drove a little faster but still within the speed limit until they were clear of the town.

Once they drove on to the unmade road, she couldn't go fast even if she wanted to—the deep corrugations made it impossible. Every time the car struck a bump, she heard his indrawn breath and wished she could go more gently. She was thankful when the cabin came in sight.

He refused her offer of help and used his crutch to get out of the car and into the cabin. She followed him, carrying her purchases. The smell of roast chicken teased at her nostrils, reminding her that she was hungry, having eaten only dry biscuits and toast this morning.

He watched in silence as she put everything away then carved the chicken and set it on to two plates, adding the fresh salad vegetables she'd bought that morning. Pointedly, she put a glass of water beside his plate and was rewarded when he took out a jar of white capsules, palmed two of them and swallowed them with the water.

She was pleased to see that he ate well, even commenting favourably on the food. 'Wait until I actually cook something,' she said. 'The twins loved my cooking, although they hated having to admit it.'

His eyes sought hers across the table. 'You miss your brothers, don't you?'

She looked away, blinking hard. 'I should. I practically brought them up.'

'I'll bet you did a damned fine job of it, too.'

Her surprised gaze flickered back to him and her face warmed with pleasure. 'Do you think so?'

'From what you've told me, there's no doubt. If you hadn't, you wouldn't have been able to leave them in your stepmother's hands and go on with your own life.'

She hadn't thought of it that way, as a job well done. 'No, I wouldn't, would I?' she echoed. It *was* partly due to her upbringing that the boys had accepted their father's remarriage so well. Why hadn't she seen it as a compliment before, rather than a rejection?

With a sudden flash of insight, she realised that that was what being a mother was all about: preparing your children to stand on their own feet. She'd done it for the twins and would one day do the same for her own baby. Her emotions, always near the surface these days, threatened to overwhelm her and she stood up briskly. 'I'll do the washing-up. You look as if you could use a rest.'

He gave her a heavy-lidded glance. 'You could be right. Leave those in the sink and I'll do them later. Go for a walk or something.'

'I might sit outside and read,' she agreed. It was obvious that he regarded his infirmity as a weakness and didn't like her witnessing it. She picked up her sun-hat and book and went to the door. 'Do you want anything before I go?'

The moment his glance rested on her full breasts, outlined in her screen-printed T-shirt, she was sorry she'd asked. The shirt had fitted perfectly when she'd left Sydney, but her blossoming figure was straining it already. 'What I want, you wouldn't care to discuss,' he said huskily.

Face flaming, she went outside, hearing his throaty laughter follow her. Damn him! He was teasing her and she had fallen for it.

But *had* he been teasing? He must have been, she thought, remembering his taunt that there was more chance of a tidal wave in Lightning Ridge, one of the driest parts of the state, than of her becoming pregnant to him. His feelings towards her were perfectly clear.

It must be her heightened emotional state that was making her so sensitive to him, she decided. She had never been so aware of a man before. Even when she had believed herself in love with Derek, he had never made her entire body tingle as if an electric current had passed through it.

Just thinking about it made her feel vibrantly alive in a way that was startlingly new to her. If she looked in a mirror now, her eyes would be burning and her skin glowing, as if she were a fever victim. In a way, she was. But it was only the baby making her overly vulnerable. She would have to be careful not to let Lachlan see how she felt—she didn't want him mistaking a pregnant woman's folly for genuine desire.

Restless with herself, she closed the book and stood up. There was one fever which *could* be controlled: opal fever. Like most miners, she'd succumbed to it with her first valuable find and kept it in check ever since with regular doses of mining activity. Why shouldn't she do a spot of prospecting while Lachlan was asleep?

Her miner's hard hat, boots and gear were stowed behind the cabin. She dressed quietly to avoid waking Lachlan, then set off for the old shaft. It would be the greatest luck to find another valuable opal so close to the first, but luck was what opal mining was all about. Of course, any gems she found would belong to Lachlan, but the excitement and satisfaction would be all hers.

The rope ladder was still in place where she had used it to help Lachlan, and she climbed down it carefully. The shaft was shallow and filled with dirt, but off it ran another shaft at right angles, leading to the cavern where she had found the first opal.

There had been so much digging in the cavern that the different levels of rock were exposed in bands to her torch beam. After a metre or so of dry, sandy material came a tightly packed layer of pinkish red sandstone, then what the miners called the steel band, a layer of opalised sandstone. It was in this layer that opals were most likely to be found.

Before Lachlan had arrived she had been working on a section of the cavern roof and she returned to it now, chipping carefully with her sharp-pointed pick, all the while watching for traces of potch, the common opal, which could lead her to the valuable stones.

She had been working steadily for over an hour with nothing to show for her efforts, when the sound of her name echoed eerily around the cavern. 'Je-nee! Je-nee!'

She edged carefully back to the intersection of the two shafts and poked her head through the hole. Lachlan's face was framed in the opening overhead. 'I'm down here,' she called.

'I can see that,' came his angry response. 'What the hell do you think you're doing?'

The vehemence in his voice alarmed her. She hadn't expected him to be so angry. 'I'm coming up,' she said, working her way into the old shaft.

She was halfway up the rope ladder when one side gave and she lurched sideways, bruising her thigh against the wall of the shaft. Only her desperate grip on the remaining rope saved her from falling down the shaft. It wasn't deep, but she could still have been injured. As it was, the rope had burned her palms.

'For heaven's sake, hang on,' Lachlan barked overhead.

He dropped all his length on to the dirt at the mouth of the shaft and stretched out his hand to her. His fingers stopped short of her straining grasp.

'I can't quite reach,' she said, straining harder.

'Yes, you can. Twist your feet around the rope. Use the knots where the rungs joined on to it as footholds. Then inch your way up to me. You must have done this in gym class when you were at school.'

She gave a shaky laugh. 'I was terrible at gym class.'

'Come on, I know you can do it.'

Gritting her teeth, she inched up the rope until their fingers touched. Seconds later his strong grip closed around her wrist. With his help she climbed the rest of the way up the rope. When she was within reach, he clasped his hands under her arms and hauled her bodily out of the shaft.

Her breathing became ragged as they clung together. She became achingly conscious of his closeness and her senses swam with the masculine aura he projected. His arms were still around her and she was aware of every sculpted muscle and sinew. She drank in the sight of him as if for the first time. Why hadn't she noticed how much of a man he was?

Her throat tightened and she swallowed convulsively as crazy thoughts chased themselves around in her head. What would it be like to be kissed by him? To have him make love to her?

She blinked the dust out of her eyes. What was she doing, letting such fairy-tale notions beguile her? Hadn't Derek taught her anything? She tensed, stepping deliberately out of the circle of his arms. 'I'm all right now, thank you.'

Thunderclouds massed in his eyes. 'All right? You damned near got yourself killed, you stupid woman.'

Adrenalin rushed through her body, but it was the healthy stimulation of anger. 'Hardly stupid. At least I *meant* to go down the shaft—I didn't fall down it.'

'Neither would I if you'd taken the proper precautions,' he threw back at her. 'But we're not discussing my behaviour. We're discussing yours and you had no business going down there.'

His fingers bit into the soft tissue of her upper arms and she squirmed in the punishing grip. 'You're hurting me. I know I shouldn't have been working your mine, but I wasn't going to steal your opals. It was something to do, that's all.'

He released her and raked stiff fingers through his hair. 'I don't give a damn about the opals—I was worried about the baby. *Now* do you see why I'm angry?'

It was her turn to be annoyed. 'I see, all right. You're more concerned about the baby than you are about me. My doctor assured me that in the early stages there's no reason to restrict my activities in any way. But that's not good enough for you because, for some reason, the baby is important to you.'

'Nonsense,' he said, turning away.

'Is it? Then why did you react so badly this morning when I asked you if you wanted children? Now you're acting as if I had deliberately put my baby at risk.' She paused, searching for the right words. 'I know you don't think I'm an attractive woman, but——'

His startled gaze raked her face. 'What makes you think I don't find you attractive? You're a beautiful woman. Your mirror must tell you so every morning.'

'You don't have to lie to make me feel better. This morning you made yourself quite clear when you said I had no chance of conceiving your child.'

'And I meant what I said.'

In exasperation she spread her hands, palms down. 'Exactly. So why try to spare my feelings now?'

He shook his head in frustration. 'I'm not trying to spare you. What I said was the simple truth.' He looked away, wrestling with himself as if he wasn't sure whether to go on or not. Finally, he looked back at her, the decision made. 'You could never conceive my child because I can't father a child by you or any other woman.'

As the reality of what he had said sank in, her face went white. She had been so sure she repelled him that it had never occurred to her to look for another explanation. 'Oh, Lachlan. I'm so sorry. I didn't know.'

His eyes were cold as he faced her. 'How could you? No one does except my ex-wife.'

And now *she* knew. The confession must have cost him dearly and she bitterly regretted forcing it from him. If only she hadn't gone on and on about children. But it was too late now. He must hate her for compelling him to bare his soul like this. 'Forgive me,' she implored. 'I had no right to pry.'

Some of the bleakness left his face. 'And I had no right to tell you what to do.'

'At least I understand why you were so angry,' she said softly.

He reached a decision. 'While you shower and change, I'll make some coffee and we'll talk. You may as well know the whole story.'

By the time she had sluiced away the white opal dust and changed into a filmy, floral caftan, he had the coffee made and a plate of biscuits set out between them. He pushed them towards her but she shook her head. 'I'm still full from lunch.'

'You don't eat much, do you?'

'Normally I do. The baby took away a lot of my appetite. I have to be careful to eat enough to stay healthy.'

His dark eyes underwent a sea change from calm to stormy before he got a grip on himself. 'Ah, yes, the baby. With the training he's getting, he'll probably grow up to be an opal miner.'

Her smile became shy. 'What makes you think it's a he?'

'Wishful thinking. Most men want their first-born to be a boy.'

He spoke almost as if the baby were his, she noticed uncomfortably. Surely he didn't think he had any claims to her child, just because he had sheltered her for a couple of nights?

His self-deprecating smile eased her mind. 'I sound as if it's my child, don't I? Now that *is* wishful thinking.'

She took a sip of the coffee. 'Are you absolutely sure it isn't possible?'

His mouth lifted in an ironic smile which made her stomach feel as if it had turned over. She suppressed the urge to go to him and try to smooth away whatever made him smile so unpleasantly. It was crazy. She had no rights where he was concerned. 'I'm sure,' he said flatly.

'Do you want to talk about it?'

'Surprisingly, I do, to you. For some reason, I get the feeling that you'll understand and won't use it as a weapon against me.'

Her gaze was filled with genuine horror. 'Why should I do any such thing?'

'My ex-wife did. When she found out that I couldn't father a child, she deliberately got herself pregnant to another man, a shearer who was passing through the district. She thought I'd be forced to divorce her then.'

'And you didn't agree?'

His hand balled into a fist. 'Lord, no! To me, a child is a gift, a pearl beyond price. I couldn't blame an innocent child for the sins of its parents, even for wickedness as great as Christine's.'

A giant hand squeezed her heart as if in a vice. 'What did she do?' she asked, her voice barely rising above a whisper.

'The doctor warned her that she could lose the child if she wasn't careful. She went horseback riding, over the roughest terrain on Orana.'

Jenny's fingers flew to her mouth as she tried to imagine herself doing such a dreadful thing. She couldn't come to grips with it. 'She lost the baby?' she said, guessing the truth from his bleak expression.

'That's right. So she won in the end. I agreed to a divorce. I knew then that there was no hope for us as a couple.'

Her hand inched towards his on the table-top, but she pulled back when she saw his face. His shuttered look locked out everything but his own inner pain.

She searched for something to say to ease his torment. Everything she could summon to mind seemed trite and useless. 'I wish I'd known before I went back down the mine,' she said at last.

He rubbed his chin, which was dusted with toast-brown stubble. 'Maybe I'm over-reacting, but you can see now why I wasn't entirely joking when I suggested we get married for the sake of your baby.'

Ice began to flow through her veins. 'It might solve your problem of an heir, but it wouldn't be my answer.'

'Why not? I could give you everything you could want, a home and a name for your child.'

'My child already *has* a name,' she all but screamed. 'I may regret what I did, but it doesn't make me want this baby any the less.'

'Yet you'd bring it into the world to live in a cabin on an opal field, with no job and no security. Can't you see how foolish you're being?'

'Maybe, but it's my life,' she said stubbornly, wishing he wouldn't paint such a bleak picture of her future, especially when she knew it was accurate. A hard knot of anguish formed in her chest. 'Why are you doing this?'

'If you'd been where I've been, seen what I've seen . . .' He tailed off as if he'd said more than he meant to.

She faced him defiantly. 'Go on. I'm listening.'

He shook his head. 'Forget it. I shouldn't have said anything.'

Apprehension flared through her but she quelled it. 'But you did, and now I want to know the rest. Why are you so worked up about me and my baby? It can't be just because you can't have your own.'

A look of such savagery came into his eyes that she was shaken. 'Very well, you asked for it. The reason I cherish children so much is because of what I saw while I was with the RAAF Number Five Squadron, stationed in the Sinai.'

She recalled Lucy saying that Lachlan had been in some peace-keeping force in the Middle East. But it wasn't with the army at all. 'You were in the Air Force?' she said in surprise.

'It's not so unusual. In the country, we learn to fly planes the way city teenagers learn to drive cars. I had my private pilot's licence as soon as I was legally old enough, at seventeen, although I could fly long before. I got my helicopter pilot's licence soon afterwards.'

'But why the Air Force? Weren't you needed to help run Orana?'

His mouth twisted into a cynical smile. 'At that time, my father didn't need anyone. I was useful as an extra pair of hands, but not to make decisions or take any responsibility. So I joined the RAAF.'

Immediately, an image of him in the smart blue uniform of an Air Force officer sprang to her mind. She could picture him at the controls of some powerful fighting machine. 'Your family must have been proud of you,' she thought aloud.

'My father didn't give a damn whether I flew crop-dusters or Iroquois helicopters,' he said tautly. 'He acted as if I'd left deliberately to flout his authority.'

'What about your mother? Don't all mothers keep pictures of their sons in uniform by their bedsides?'

He shrugged. 'I suppose she was proud of me. But her letters were full of the doings of the local girls and what wonderful wives they'd make, or news of Kate and her family. I was left in no doubt where my real duty lay.'

A shudder ran through him and she wished she had the right to comfort him. Didn't his parents know how much anguish their attitude had caused him? 'But you did come back and take over,' she reminded him.

'I couldn't stay in the Air Force after Sinai,' he said harshly, his eyes regaining their shuttered look. The silence stretched between them as he wrestled with his memories. He blinked and cleared his throat. 'Hell, you may as well know it all. A detachment from my squadron was assigned to serve with the United Nations Emergency Forces. When we weren't flying Iroquois, some of us visited the refugee camps on the Egypt-Sinai border. We thought we could make a difference to their plight.'

The turbulence in his expression alarmed her. What had he seen in those places? 'You needn't go on,' she suggested gently.

His dark glance mocked her. 'Getting too rough for you, is it?'

'No!' She only wanted to shield him from memories which were obviously painful, not to protect herself.

The hardness about his eyes and mouth made her think he was reliving his memories, not just re-counting them to her. 'It gets worse,' he said in a clipped, metallic voice. 'In the camps, families of sixteen people lived in two-roomed tin shacks. Kids played in garbage dumps. A family of ten could expect to lose half their children to cholera, typhus and tuberculosis. And do you know the worst of it?'

She could only shake her head. 'No.'

'There was nothing I could do. As fast as we brought food or medicine, it was swallowed up by a tide of humanity which there was no stemming. The more we did, the more there was screaming to be done.'

Unable even to imagine what he had seen, she shuddered. 'Those poor people.'

A glint of anger lit his gaze. 'Those poor people have been fighting each other since Biblical times. They chose their own course. But the children had no choice. Yet they suffered and died equally. Nobody seemed to care.'

Jenny longed to tell him that it was all right, his presence in that far-off land meant that *he* cared. He didn't think it was enough. She understood now why he was so appalled at Derek's behaviour. For a man to abandon his own child was anathema to Lachlan. He had seen too many children die, unable to help them. His own child would be different, but he would never know that joy. 'You said you couldn't stay in the RAAF after that. Was it because of what you'd seen?' she prompted when the silence went on too long.

He came back to her slowly. 'No, although it nearly broke most of us. The end came when our base was attacked by terrorists using a new kind of chemical weapon.'

It was said so matter-of-factly that it took her a moment to absorb the full horror of his statement. He had been subjected to a deadly chemical which had destroyed his ability to father children. 'Oh, Lachlan,' she breathed, her mind numb with shock.

He shrugged, but it didn't disguise the shudder which shook him. 'I only caught the fringe of the barrage. I didn't think I'd suffered any ill-effects until Christine and I found we couldn't have a family. Then we put two and two together, but it was too late. Christine wanted out and used it as her excuse.'

Jenny was shocked into immobility by his revelations. How many people saw Lachlan Frost as the privileged son of a wealthy grazing family and envied him? She had a feeling he hadn't shared his experiences with very many people—she might even be the first. Why had he chosen her to confide in? It must be because of the baby, not because of Jenny herself. He had made it clear that the child was his first concern. The thought was oddly painful but, she had to admit, realistic.

'I'm glad you told me,' she said, sounding more choked than she intended. 'I promise I'll take care of myself *and* the baby from now on.'

Something unfathomable gleamed in his velvet gaze. 'But you don't have to. I can take care of you both if you'll let me.' He stood up and moved around to her side of the table, his expression hardening suddenly. 'I know what's wrong. Because of what I've told you, you think I couldn't be a husband to you, don't you?'

It had never even crossed her mind, and she shook her head wildly from side to side as adrenalin pumped through her body. He was so close to her that his warmth radiated towards her.

Anxious to meet him on his level, she stood up. Being seated while he towered over her made her feel too much at a disadvantage. 'I don't think any such thing,' she stammered. Standing up had been the wrong move, she realised as soon as she came up against the hard wall of his chest.

His arms encircled her. 'All the same, I'd like to put your mind at rest.'

CHAPTER FIVE

THIS maelstrom of thoughts and feelings was hardly rest, Jenny thought as her heart began to beat a frenetic tattoo. It had to be the shock of finding herself in Lachlan's arms. It couldn't be because he was about to kiss her and, in spite of everything, she wanted him to, could it?

His eyes locked with hers, drawing her into them as if into a bottomless pool. His hands scorched her through the thin caftan. Slowly, ever so slowly, they slid down her back, sending shivers of electric pleasure all the way down her spine. Ignoring her mental command to be still, her body arched against him, responding of its own accord to his touch in ways which defied common sense.

'You see? I can make you want me,' he whispered. 'And I can make love to you in ways you've never dreamed possible.'

Oh, lord, she was dreaming of it now, she found to her eternal shame. He was playing a concerto of such wild, sweet music up and down her spine that her bones felt liquid. He could shape her to his heart's desire and her only protest would be when he stopped.

When he bent his head to kiss her, she shaped her mouth to his willingly, raising herself on tiptoe to meet him more than halfway. The pressure on her lips was like a kiss of fire. Answering flames leapt inside her, heating her to the very core of her being.

Distantly, alarm bells rang in her head. What was she doing, behaving so wantonly in his arms? At least with Derek she had had the excuse of utter loneliness. With Lachlan, there was only desire such as she had never known in her wildest dreams. It was only by reminding herself that he wanted her because of the baby, not because he found her desirable, that she managed to pull free and put the width of the table between them.

As she cowered there, tremors still shaking her, he regarded her with wry amusement. 'I see I've made my point.'

He meant that he was still a man in every way which mattered, and she had no breath to deny it. The proof surged through her with the force of a live current. She gripped the table-edge to steady herself. 'You've made your point all right. You want an heir so badly that you'll use any trick in the book to make it possible.'

'I know quite a few which aren't in the book,' he said mildly. 'But that isn't the point, is it? What passed between us just now has nothing to do with a child. You know it as well as I do.'

She shook her head. He wanted her to believe it, but the truth was too obvious. 'Nothing passed between us, as you put it. You caught me off guard, that's all. I'll be better prepared next time.'

His eyes gleamed. 'Will you? Even if next time is now?'

No amount of preparation would insure her against him! Her response defied all reason, but

she was *not* going to let it rule her. She took a wary
step backwards. 'There won't *be* a next time,' she
said, lifting her chin. 'I'm leaving the Ridge tomorrow and going back to Sydney where I belong.'

He slammed his hands, palms down, against the
table, making her jump. 'This is where you belong,
whether you admit it or not.'

Deliberately, she misinterpreted his words. 'This
is your cabin, as you took pains to point out.'

Exasperation and anger chased each other across
his rugged features. 'I wasn't talking about the
cabin, as well you know. I mean Lightning Ridge,
the opal country. It's in your blood.'

She could hardly deny it. 'I know, but——'

'And you can't leave me to fend by myself with
this foot,' he pressed home his advantage.

Although he hadn't used the crutch since
lunchtime, she had noticed that he kept his weight
on his uninjured foot, limping heavily on the short
walk from the mineshaft to the cabin. 'You
managed to come looking for me, so it can't be all
that bad,' she said.

'It's getting better but I doubt if I can drive yet.'
Dropping on to the chair, he lifted his foot on to
a stool, wincing as he did so. 'Check it yourself and
see whether or not I'm playing possum.'

In her present sensitised state, she would have
preferred not to touch him at all, but she had
thrown down the gauntlet. If she backed away now,
he would have no doubt about his effect on her.
She had no choice but to kneel in front of him and
go to work on the bandage.

Her fingers shook as she unwound the cloth, which was thick with dust from the mine. He eased his trouser leg up his calf and, with each touch, the back of her hand grazed the hair-strewn skin. She was torn between wanting to be in his arms, and needing to escape his compelling power over her. He was a flame and she was a moth, drawn into his circle of light no matter how far or fast she tried to flutter away.

The bandage snaked to the floor and she sucked in a sharp breath. Lachlan's ankle wasn't badly swollen any more, but around the bone was an ugly mass of blue-black bruising. She probed it gently with her fingers and he gasped. Looking up, she found his eyes fixed on her. 'I'm sorry. I didn't mean to hurt you.'

'But you will, won't you?' he said with strange detachment. 'You alone have the power.'

'I'm being as careful as I can,' she insisted, but had the uncanny feeling that he meant something else. How could she possibly hurt him? It didn't make sense. Unless he meant she could do it by hurting the baby, which he must know by now she couldn't do.

She went to fetch a fresh bandage and the anti-biotic cream the doctor had prescribed to ward off infection. As she massaged the cream into his ankle she tried to fix her mind on other things, but her throat was tight with nameless longing by the time she finished. It was an effort to speak normally. 'Is that better?'

'Much, thank you.' His voice had deepened, too. 'Do you still think I should drive myself home?'

She was forced to be honest. 'No. I'll drive you back to Orana tomorrow.' Before he could say anything, she added quickly, 'Then I'll drive to Walgett and get a room there. It will be too late to drive back to Sydney by then, but I can get an early start the following day.'

He remained silent, brooding. She decided to play her final card. 'I've also decided we can't share the bed tonight. The sleeping-bag will be perfectly comfortable for one night.'

'Then I'll be the one to use it,' he insisted.

She felt like throwing something at him. 'You can't with your ankle in that condition.'

He gave a long-suffering sigh. 'Then we're back to our original arrangement. Unless you want to spend the whole night arguing about it?'

If she told him how she really wanted to spend the whole night, he would be astonished, she thought, surprising herself with the admission. 'I'll use the sleeping-bag on the bed,' she compromised, banishing her errant thoughts.

He shrugged. 'Suit yourself. I imagine you usually do anyway.'

He remained distant and moody for the rest of the evening, picking at the ham and eggs she prepared for supper and finally pushing the plate away. 'Can I get you anything else?' she asked.

'No, thanks. I'm not very hungry. I think I'll turn in early.'

She had hoped to be the first one to retire, so she could be asleep or at least pretending before he joined her, but he had forestalled her. The sounds of his undressing for bed tantalised her as she cleared away the dishes and washed them, although she deliberately clattered them loudly in the stainless-steel sink. By the time she had finished, he was stretched out full-length on the double bed. His eyes were shut.

With Lachlan taking up half of it, the bed seemed to have shrunk since the previous night. It would be difficult to avoid touching him as they slept. Still, she knew that if she tried to unroll the sleeping-bag on the floor he was quite capable of putting her to bed himself, injury or no injury. With a resigned sigh, she unrolled the sleeping-bag beside him.

He appeared to be sleeping, but Jenny approached cautiously. 'Lachlan?' There was no answer. She eased her nightgown out from under her pillow and backed away. He didn't stir and she felt safe to pull her caftan off. Her reflection, revealed in ecru lace bra and panties, caught her attention and she paused. Was it her imagination or was there a slight swelling above her bikini-line? She was well into her third month, so it was possible. In the mirror, her reflection returned her dreamy smile. Her baby already looked human although it weighed no more than half an ounce; by now the head, arms, legs and even fingernails were fully formed, according to her doctor.

Wonder flooded through her and she splayed her fingers across her stomach. Her baby! The fantasy was fast becoming reality.

At the same time, a feeling of dread assailed her. Was she doing the right thing, bearing a child alone, with no father and no real security? Lachlan's accusations weighed heavily on her mind. Her gaze flew to him. If she agreed to his proposal, her worries would be over. Despite her harsh words at the pool, she was sure he would make an ideal father. Materially, his family would want for nothing. But was it enough? What about love? Surely it wasn't wishing for the moon to want her baby's father to love her as well?

'So it is true. Pregnancy *does* make a woman more beautiful.'

'What?' Lachlan's lazy comment made her realise that he wasn't asleep at all, probably never had been. He watched her from under hooded lids, his expression dark and unreadable. She reached for her nightgown and pulled it quickly over her head, hoping that he hadn't witnessed the moment of communion with her unborn child. She didn't want him to guess what she'd been thinking.

Putting out the light, she wriggled her way into the sleeping-bag, trying not to touch Lachlan as he lay beside her. When she was safely cocooned, she slid the front-fastening zipper all the way up to her chin. It was stifling, but no part of her touched him.

'Aren't you hot in that thing?' he said into the darkness.

'No, thank you. I'm fine.' How primly Victorian she sounded. And she *was* hot. A tiny trickle of perspiration wended its way between her breasts.

She endured it until Lachlan's breathing become slow and even. Then she eased the zipper all the way down. Blissful coolness wafted over her skin. She worked her shoulders clear of the bag and immediately felt better. At least she wouldn't suffocate during the night.

Lachlan stirred in his sleep and their hips touched. Instantly, something stirred inside Jenny, an echo of the yearnings she remembered from her childhood. It was a *wanting*, without being able to say what she wanted.

A neediness she hadn't known she owned flooded through her. But what did she need so badly? She only knew that it reached to the depths of her being and made her feel more alone than she had ever done.

Wetness seeped from beneath her long lashes as understanding came. Not since her mother died had she felt truly *loved*. Her father must have loved her, but he didn't show it. Derek's love was a cruel pretence. Linda resented her. Even the twins loved her selfishly, for what she had done for them. It was typical of children, but it hurt, nevertheless.

Angrily, she dashed the tears away. It was just as well she was going back to Sydney tomorrow. Self-pity was a poor reason for marriage and she was in danger of giving in to it if she stayed. For the baby's sake, she tried to calm her mind so she could get her much-needed rest, but it was a long time before she managed to fall asleep.

Her dreams were troubled. She found herself in an arctic wasteland with nothing but snow and ice as far as she could see. A baby was crying. Her baby. She fought her way through the drifts, trying to reach her child. Shivers swept through her and her teeth chattered. 'Cold, so cold,' she moaned.

'Jenny, wake up.'

The dream faded slowly but she was still cold. In the grey light of dawn, Lachlan's face loomed above her, his eyes dark with concern. 'Wake up, it's only a dream.'

She wrapped her arms tightly around her body. 'It was freezing where I was.'

A faint smile lit his face. 'You kicked off your sleeping-bag. Your limbs are like ice.'

He pulled her against his chest and his body heat warmed her. It was no more than a comforting gesture, but every nerve-ending leapt to vibrant life. When she tried to push him away he held her irresistibly, the struggle bringing them closer until she was enveloped by his warm, masculine aura.

Unable to fight him, she tried to relax, telling herself the moment meant nothing, at least to Lachlan. He had no idea that his touch sent arrows of desire shooting to her core. Fiery warmth licked at her limbs, not from the transfer of body heat he intended, but from her own flagrant responses which threatened to consume her.

She was unaware of reaching out until her hands linked behind the firm column of his neck. His hair tangled around her fingers as she eased his head towards her. His lips hovered tantalisingly near her mouth.

Then abruptly her hands were freed and he pushed her away. A foot of bed-space yawned between them. Roughly, he pulled a blanket up and covered her, tucking it around her to exclude himself.

Imprisoned by the blanket, she lay stiffly, trying to absorb what had just happened. His embrace had been warm and welcoming until she'd tried to return it. Then it had been withdrawn. The reason was obvious: he didn't want her as a woman, only as the mother of the child he was unable to have. It was a bitter lesson but she had learned it now—he wouldn't need to repeat it.

She tried to settle her mind by making a plan to follow once she got back to Sydney, but her tired brain refused to deal with anything beyond saying goodbye to Lachlan.

She didn't expect to sleep again but somehow she did, waking to find bright sunlight flooding through the cabin. Still swathed in the blanket, she struggled free of it. The day was already hot in contrast to the cool night. Recalling Lachlan's remedy for the cold made her flush. What a fool she had made of herself last night, mistaking his gesture of comfort for something more. Thank goodness she was leaving today, before she made any more such mistakes.

'Good, you're awake.' Lachlan appeared at her bedside with a steaming cup in one hand and a plate in the other.

She smiled awkwardly. 'What's this?'

'Dry biscuits and weak, milky tea. Correct?'

'Perfect, but you didn't have to.' She sat up and accepted the offerings. Surprisingly, her stomach was much more settled this morning. The doctor had assured her that the nausea would disappear altogether soon. She sipped the tea and nibbled on the biscuits.

Lachlan watched her critically, then sat down on the side of the bed. 'About last night——'

'It's all right,' she interrupted. 'I knew it was a mistake from the beginning.'

She meant that she should have stuck to her guns and slept in the sleeping-bag on the floor, but he chose his own interpretation. 'So you *were* half asleep and didn't know what you were doing. I was afraid so.' He sounded curiously disappointed.

She should have been relieved to have him blame her behaviour on her sleep-drugged state, but her insides twisted in protest. She *had* known what she was doing. He was the one who had rejected her. He was trying to be kind but she wished he wouldn't dress it up. He didn't want her, only what she could give him.

She handed him the cup and plate. 'Would you excuse me? I'll get dressed now.'

'There's no need to get up until you're ready.'

A wave of weariness washed over her. It was tempting to plead illness and lie back, but why postpone the inevitable? The sooner she drove him home to Orana, the sooner she could take her leave. She couldn't stay on his terms, and they were all he was offering.

Breakfast was a silent affair. Busy with her turbulent thoughts, Jenny noticed that Lachlan was also preoccupied. No doubt he could see his chance at fatherhood slipping away again. She was under no illusion that her departure meant anything else to him.

With the politeness of strangers they agreed to leave his car at the cabin for one of his staff to collect later, transferring his luggage to her car for the drive to Orana.

Replenishing her petrol supply at Lightning Ridge, Jenny took a last look around the small community. She felt a pang. It should have been her home until the baby came, but instead she was leaving it, perhaps never to return. Nothing had turned out the way she'd planned it.

'Hello, you look a bit down. What's the matter?'

Lucy Baxter came up to her and they hugged delightedly. 'I'm returning to Sydney today,' Jenny told her. It was hard to keep her emotions out of her voice.

Lucy frowned. 'I wish you'd told me in time to arrange a farewell dinner.'

'I was going to call you,' Jenny assured her friend. 'But I don't want a fuss.'

Lucy nodded. 'I know how you feel.' She looked around. 'I passed your car at the petrol pump. Isn't your passenger Lachlan Frost?'

Jenny ducked her head, afraid that her flustered expression would give Lucy ideas. 'He hurt his ankle. I agreed to drop him at Orana before I started for home.'

'Very public-spirited of you.' Lucy's smile widened. 'So you accepted his offer of a drink after all?'

Why had she told Lucy about that first encounter with Lachlan in the bar? Now she was reading all the wrong things into the situation. 'No, I didn't,' she said firmly. 'I'm helping him out, that's all.'

Lucy nodded gravely. 'Of course you are. Never mind that Orana and Sydney lie in opposite directions.'

Confusion clouded Jenny's mind. Whatever she said, Lucy was determined to misread it. 'I must go,' she said in desperation. 'I'll write to you from Sydney.'

'Or invite me to visit Orana,' Lucy put in with a huge wink.

'You're impossible!' Jenny wailed. But Lucy was already walking away. Well, she would have to believe her own eyes when the next letter she received from Jenny was postmarked Sydney, Jenny consoled herself. She was not—repeat, not—staying at Orana.

With her first sight of Orana Homestead, however, her resolve began to waver. The property was a good two-hour drive from Lightning Ridge. Once on Orana land, she had to drive for another forty minutes over corrugated dirt roads between black-soil paddocks to reach the house. She was starting to think they would never get there when the road crested a ridge and there was the homestead ahead of them.

With its corrugated steel roof and deep verandas sheltering the front door, it was strikingly Australian in character. The handmade cream bricks and the strong twin pillars of the chimneys made her nostalgic for the sound of an axe chopping wood for the stove, the buzz of insects on a lazy summer night, and the sound of fly-screen doors slamming behind childish feet.

It was crazy but she had an instant, almost overwhelming sense of coming home. Before she set foot on the wooden veranda, she knew that the cane swing-seat would creak when pushed to and fro. She could almost have sketched the layout of the rooms. As she stood, mesmerised, in front of the house, Lachlan came up behind her. 'Is anything the matter?'

'No,' she said dreamily. 'Everything's perfect.'

And it was. The leaded front door opened on to a wide central hallway which extended for the full width of the house. Off it were large, airy rooms with beautiful furnishings and delicate pressed-metal ceilings.

She followed Lachlan along the hallway to the back of the house where, he informed her, the original servants' quarters had been converted into guest suites. The windows of these rooms looked inwards, to a cobbled courtyard. The outer walls had no windows, only narrow gunports where the property had been defended against Aboriginal attacks in colonial times.

'This is the best guest room,' he said, opening yet another door. 'I want you to have it.'

Her breath caught in her throat. Never had she seen a more charming room, more perfectly restored in tune with its period. A magnificent brass bedstead filled the centre of the room, covered with an antique lace spread. A solid cedar chest and dressing-table completed the furnishings and a corner table held a washbasin and water jug.

'I thought you said the property needs renovating,' she said almost accusingly to him.

'The main living area still does. I've managed to restore these rooms myself, but I haven't had a chance to tackle the living- and dining-rooms yet. Will you help me, Jenny?'

She was aware of his dark-eyed gaze on her but didn't trust herself to look at him. He would see in her eyes that she had fallen in love with Orana the moment she'd crossed the threshold. Leaving now would be like tearing out a part of her heart.

Leaving Orana or leaving Lachlan Frost? she asked herself. The two were becoming blurred in her mind. This was where he had been born and raised—staying here meant staying with him. The first she could cope with, the second, she wasn't so sure, especially knowing that he would never have invited her but for the baby.

Still, she wavered. The strange sense of belonging tugged at her as she looked around. 'I don't know,' she agonised.

'Come and see the rest of the house,' he coaxed. For a second, his arm rested on her shoulder as he guided her back into the hall. It was enough to send a sharp stab of sensation through her. She jerked free of his hand. He dropped it to his side. 'I'm sorry, did I touch a nerve?'

'Yes.' The admission was more true than he could possibly imagine. From first meeting, he had touched every nerve she possessed, sensitising her to him in some mystical way. It threatened to rob her of her power to act, to decide anything for herself or her child. If she stayed, it could only get worse.

Numbly, she preceded him down the hall and into a vast living-room. It had a dark Georgian atmosphere which she hated immediately. Although the windows were large and the ceiling high, the effect was gloomy. Here, she *could* make a difference. Ideas flooded into her mind, begging for expression, until she stemmed them with a gesture of dismay. The house was mesmerising her as well, willing her to stay to please its charismatic owner. 'All right, all right!' she said aloud.

He gave her a curious look. 'I didn't say anything.'

'No, but I know what you're thinking.'

'Do you, Jenny? I doubt it.' His voice was soft, caressing. In this setting he looked less like a modern-day farmer and more like a colonial aristocrat. It was easy to picture him as his ancestor of a century before, fighting off bush-rangers or marauding natives who threatened his home. He spoke, breaking into her thoughts. 'I was thinking what an ideal mistress you'd make for Orana. In a bonnet and Victorian gown, you would look perfectly at home here.'

She swallowed as a lump came into her throat. 'I was thinking the same about you,' she confessed. 'Do you believe in reincarnation?'

'Do you think we shared another life?' She nodded and his eyes narrowed. 'Whether we did or not, I want us to share this one. You know it, don't you?'

'Yes.' For all the wrong reasons, she added to herself. 'So you see why I can't possibly stay.'

'Even if I let you dictate the terms? No strings, if you prefer it that way?'

It was how she wanted it, so why did his suggestion send waves of disappointment through her?

'You promise?' she asked, half hoping he would refuse so she could leave now, before it was too late. Too late for what, she couldn't say.

'I promise. If you stay, it's on your terms.'

He wasn't going to pressure her into intimacy just because he wanted an heir. She could stay and work on this glorious house in perfect security. It should have pleased her but her mind rejected the easy bargain. How could it work when he affected her so strongly already? She was forced to admire his cleverness. He *knew* the effect he had on her, and he was so sure she would be unable to resist her own clamouring needs that she would come to him of her own accord. Then he could claim both her and the child, by default.

She meant to refuse but, somehow, the words came out as, 'Yes, I'll stay, on my terms.'

He executed a mock bow. 'Your wish is my command. I'll have your luggage taken to your room.'

'Thank you.' A sudden burst of exhilaration surged through her. She had burned her bridges but she was wildly, foolishly glad. He might only want her here because of the baby, but the knowledge wasn't enough to dampen the pleasure of working here with Lachlan, day after day.

Tyres crunched on the ironstone gravel driveway and Lachlan limped to the window, pulling back one of the heavy red velvet drapes. 'Company?' she asked curiously.

'A neighbourly visit,' he said in an odd tone. 'You go ahead and settle in while I do the honours.' Leaning on his crutch, he went outside.

She was about to return to the guest wing when something drew her to the window. The sunlight was dazzling in contrast to the cool, dark interior and it took her eyes a moment to adjust.

Lachlan rested his back against a veranda post. A low-slung maroon sports car was parked in the driveway. From it emerged a diminutive blonde woman with the most breathtaking figure Jenny had ever set eyes on. Every curve was revealed to perfection in a cream silk jumpsuit cinched by a wide leather belt. Lachlan had described her as a neighbour, but she looked more like a fashion model. When she approached the veranda, Jenny noted unhappily that she wore no rings on her flawlessly manicured hands.

Aware that she shouldn't be spying on them, Jenny couldn't seem to tear her eyes away. The woman lifted her face and gave Lachlan a radiant smile. 'Lord, I've missed you, darling.'

'Good to see you, Mandy,' came Lachlan's warm reply. Jenny couldn't see his face but his head was tilted towards the woman.

With quicksilver steps, Mandy flung herself into Lachlan's arms. Jenny waited long enough to see him return the embrace then pushed herself away from the window, feeling as if someone had just stabbed her. So this was where Lachlan loved. Thinking of the woman's luminous beauty, Jenny understood now why he had offered her everything but his heart.

CHAPTER SIX

A KNOCK on the bedroom door jolted Jenny out of her reverie. It was Lachlan. 'I wanted to let you know that we have a guest for dinner,' he informed her. 'Amanda Farmer is my neighbour to the west. She's chairing the sesquicentenary committee. Her property, Tillaron, was settled about the same time as Orana so she's got the whole valley to take part in the celebrations. You two should have a lot in common.'

More than he knew, Jenny thought with a pang. The proprietorial way Amanda had greeted him wasn't lost on her—nor was his use of the other woman's nickname. The only aspect which puzzled her was why Lachlan didn't simply marry Amanda. Intuition told her that it wasn't for lack of interest on Amanda's side.

'You're being catty,' she told her reflection as she got ready for dinner. She didn't even know Amanda Farmer, yet she was passing judgements about her. She resolved to make an effort to be friendly during dinner.

The resolution didn't prevent her from taking special pains with her dress and make-up, although she told herself it was because they were back in civilisation again, not out of any misguided competitiveness.

Swirling in front of the mirror, she inspected the results. Her drop-waisted dress, with its cap sleeves, full skirt and insets of vanilla lace contrasting with the iris-printed silk crêpe, flattered her.

Sideways on, the soft material camouflaged her blooming figure, although not for much longer. Already she could feel tension in her clothes. But for now she could wear what she liked and she determined to enjoy it.

The dress was a favourite, purchased to celebrate the completion of the Hunter Valley commission, for which she had received a very good fee. Now she was glad that she had splurged. She couldn't imagine Amanda Farmer skimping on clothes.

Gold hoop earrings and high-heeled navy pumps completed the outfit. She took a deep breath. She was as ready as she would ever be.

When she joined Lachlan and Amanda in the living-room, a woman whom Jenny guessed to be a housekeeper was handing drinks around. 'Mineral water for me, thank you,' she told the woman when the tray was offered to her.

'Jenny, this is Amanda Farmer from Tillaron,' Lachlan explained when the three of them were alone again. 'Jenny is an expert on historical restoration,' he added for Amanda's benefit.

Amanda's eyebrows rose slightly. 'Lachlan was telling me how you two met. Wasn't it lucky that of all the opal mines available, you adopted one whose owner needed help with a restoration project?'

'You make it sound as if I did it on purpose,' Jenny said, forcing herself to smile and remember her resolution. 'I honestly believed that the mine belonged to my uncle who left it to me.'

'Oh, yes, Lou Cameron.' She gave a disdainful sniff. 'We all know what *he* was like.'

Lachlan moved between them. 'Shall we go in to dinner? Mrs Napier has gone to a lot of trouble, she tells me.'

'She's been telling you that since you were a boy,' Amanda said, laughing. 'Don't you know by now, it's a ploy to get you to eat what's put in front of you?'

His laughter joined hers. 'I know, but I hate to spoil her fun.' He turned to Jenny. 'Davina Napier was my father's housekeeper. When my sister Kate and I were kids, we had running battles with her over food. She invariably won, and likes to think she still does.'

There was no mistaking his affection for the elderly housekeeper. Jenny felt a stab of envy for the woman's place in his life. What would it be like to have his total acceptance and unstinting affection? It wasn't something she was likely to find out.

Even telling herself so didn't soften the impact of seeing him with Amanda at dinner. Although they included her in their conversation, it was mostly about people she didn't know, neighbouring properties and scandals which were foreign to her. She could play only a small part. She couldn't help wondering if Amanda was deliberately excluding her.

Amanda reminded her of Linda. Jenny had the same sense of poaching on another's territory and was equally at a loss what to do about it. With

NO RISK, NO OBLIGATION TO BUY...NOW OR EVER!

GUARANTEED

PLAY "ROLL A DOUBLE" AND GET AS MANY AS SIX GIFTS!

HERE'S HOW TO PLAY:

1. Peel off label from front cover. Place it in space provided at right. With a coin, carefully scratch off the silver dice. This makes you eligible to receive one or more free books, and possibly other gifts, depending on what is revealed beneath the scratch-off area.

2. You'll receive brand-new Harlequin Romance® novels. When you return this card, we'll rush you the books and gifts you qualify for ABSOLUTELY FREE!

3. Then, if we don't hear from you, every month we'll send you 6 additional novels to read and enjoy. You can return them and owe nothing, but if you decide to keep them, you'll pay only $2.24 per book—a savings of 51¢ each off the cover price.

4. When you subscribe to the Harlequin Reader Service®, you'll also get our newsletter, as well as additional free gifts from time to time.

5. You must be completely satisfied. You may cancel at any time simply by sending us a note or a shipping statement marked ''cancel'' or by returning any shipment to us at our expense.

You'll look like a million dollars when you wear this elegant necklace! It's a generous 20 inches long and each link is double-soldered for strength and durability.

"ROLL A DOUBLE!"

PLACE LABEL HERE

SCRATCH HERE

SEE CLAIM CHART BELOW

116 CIH ACJZ

YES! I have placed my label from the front cover into the space provided above and scratched off the silver dice. Please rush me the free book(s) and gift(s) that I am entitled to. I understand that I am under no obligation to purchase any books, as explained on the opposite page.

NAME

ADDRESS _____ APT.

CITY _____ STATE _____ ZIP CODE

CLAIM CHART

 4 FREE BOOKS PLUS FREE 20" NECKLACE PLUS MYSTERY BONUS GIFT

3 FREE BOOKS PLUS BONUS GIFT

 2 FREE BOOKS

CLAIM NO. 37-829

HARLEQUIN "NO RISK" GUARANTEE

- You're not required to buy a single book—ever!
- You must be completely satisfied or you may cancel at any time simply by sending us a note or a shipping statement marked "cancel" or by returning any shipment to us at our cost. Either way, you will receive no more books; you'll have no obligation to buy.
- The free book(s) and gift(s) you claimed on this "Roll A Double" offer remain yours to keep no matter what you decide.

If offer card is missing, please write to:
Harlequin Reader Service, 3010 Walden Ave., P.O. Box 1867, Buffalo, N.Y. 14269-1867

Linda, the solution had been to move out. The opal mine had been her backstop—without it, her options were limited. Whether Amanda liked it or not, she had little choice but to stay.

Lachlan spoke to her again and she looked blankly at him. 'I'm sorry?'

'I said all this local gossip must be boring you. Your reaction proves my point.'

'I'm not bored, truly,' she attempted to reassure him. 'I suppose I'll get to know everyone if I'm here for very long.' Now why had she added a rider? Was it to subtly reassure Amanda that she had nothing to worry about? She leaned forward, remembering a snatch of the earlier conversation. 'For example, who is Grant?'

'Grant is Amanda's son,' Lachlan said, earning a look of disapproval from the other woman.

Jenny couldn't hide her surprise. 'Your son?' Her gaze went to Amanda's ringless left hand.

'I'm a widow,' Amanda said, colouring prettily. 'My husband, Steven was killed in a bushfire on our property three years ago.'

'I'm so sorry.' Jenny's response was automatic.

'It's all right, you didn't know. Grant is away at boarding-school most of the time.' She made a face. 'He's only ten and already he's made up his mind to be a scientist with the CSIRO. I always hoped——'

Lachlan's hand covered Amanda's in a comforting gesture. 'You hoped he would grow up to take over Tillaron, I know. But he has a powerful intellect. He'll be a brilliant scientist one day.'

'Yes, he will. But what will happen to the property with no one to carry it on?'

Jenny held her breath, waiting for Lachlan to say that their marriage would unite Orana and Tillaron. Instead, he looked uncomfortable. 'You know my thoughts on the subject, Mandy. It's old ground by now.'

Had he proposed to Amanda and been refused? It was hard to imagine, given the signals Jenny was picking up from the other woman. She decided to change the subject. None of it was her business anyway.

'I understand that you're arranging the local historical celebrations,' she said over-brightly. 'I'd like to hear more about the occasion.'

'As a history buff, I suppose you would,' Amanda said without much enthusiasm. Jenny could almost see her upbringing at work as she pulled herself together. 'Long before opals were found around here, my family and Lachlan's were here as free settlers, receiving the land as a grant from the Government. In 1835 our ancestors helped to put down a convict uprising. As a reward, they were given more land, creating Tillaron and Orana as they are today. By the nineteen-hundreds, when opal mining started, we'd been here for seventy years. So it's really a local celebration. Much of the valley is still in the hands of the original families.'

'It's an impressive history,' Jenny agreed. 'Restoring Orana to its original style is a wonderful way to mark the occasion.'

'Thanks, it was my idea,' Amanda said. 'Each generation added bits to the original house until it was unrecognisable, but Lachlan ferreted out enough of the plans and inventories to get as close to the original as possible.'

Jenny's eyes shone as she looked at him. 'I can't wait to see those documents.'

His answering gaze was good-humoured, as if her enthusiasm struck a chord in him. 'We'll go over them before you start work.'

'It will give me much more to go on than paint scrapings and guesswork.'

'Did you form any first impressions after our guided tour?' he asked.

She hesitated. 'What you've done with the servants' quarters is stunning. But...'

'The living-room bothers you?'

'Yes. I need to study the room in more detail but the Georgian style feels all wrong.'

'What would you suggest?' Amanda asked. Her glance challenged Jenny to prove her credentials.

Jenny thought for a moment. 'It's only a first impression, but the light colour of the timber and the hand-carved wall-panelling suggests early Victorian. If the panelling is original?' She flashed a questioning look to Lachlan.

He nodded. 'It's listed on the inventories. The original colour scheme is described as magenta and gold.'

'Of course! Around the eighteen-fifties, aniline dyes were just coming into use. Colours like magenta, dark green and purple were used in decorating for the first time. The furnishings should be Victorian to match the architectural period.'

'I thought Victorian furniture was all dark and gloomy with frills over the table-legs,' Amanda muttered.

Jenny warmed to her subject. 'Not necessarily. In decorating, there are three Victorian eras, co-inciding with what happened during her reign. The prudish time came later, when Queen Victoria's husband Albert died and she went into mourning for three years.'

Amanda gave her a look of grudging admir-ation. 'You really do know your stuff, don't you?'

Feeling as if she had passed a test, Jenny began to relax, happy to talk about her work and the ideas for Orana which were taking shape in her mind.

Several times she felt Lachlan's eyes on her, but when she looked up his glance slid away. Catching sight of herself in a wall mirror, she saw that her cheeks were flushed and her eyes bright, but it was with enthusiasm for her subject. It couldn't be the reason for Lachlan's intense interest. Maybe he was trying to make up for excluding her from the con-versation earlier.

It was late by the time they left the table. Amanda looked at the clock and gave a shriek of dismay. 'You could stay the night and drive home in the morning,' Lachlan suggested.

Amanda gave Jenny a look of unmistakable triumph. I can go or stay as I choose, her look seemed to say. If she stayed, whose room would she sleep in? Jenny found herself wondering with a feeling akin to pain.

'No, I should go,' Amanda decided. 'The committee meets at my home tomorrow morning. I want to be bright-eyed when they arrive.'

With eyes as dark as raisins in a flawless peaches and cream complexion, it was hard to imagine Amanda ever looking other than bright-eyed, Jenny thought. She really was a stunning-looking woman. Lachlan evidently thought so, because he gave her a playful hug. 'You could dance all night and still be bright-eyed next morning,' he assured Amanda.

Her smile widened. 'Flatterer.' But she looked pleased as she gazed up at Lachlan.

A stab of something she recognised unwillingly as envy pierced Jenny. Amanda was in love with him—it showed in how she looked at him and in her sinuous body language. He must see it. Was he in love with Amanda? He was easy and friendly towards her; he had kissed her with a warmth which took Jenny's breath away. Oh, no, was he in love with Amanda?

Her vision blurred as she took hasty leave of them and made her way to the guest wing. She didn't want to witness any more loving scenes between them.

She was undressed and showering when the reason for her behaviour hit her with the force of a cyclone. She hated seeing Amanda in Lachlan's arms because that was where *she* wanted to be. She was in love with Lachlan herself.

She sagged against the tiled wall of the shower, letting her tears mingle with the cascade of water. Why hadn't she seen this coming? His instant impact on her in the bar at Lightning Ridge, coupled with her own electric responses, should have warned her she was in danger of falling for him. Yet his interest in her began and ended with the baby. It was hopeless.

No, it wasn't. Her jaw firmed on the thought. She needed a home and a job and Orana provided both. For her baby's sake, she had to see this through even if it meant putting her heart back together at the end of it.

Pretend he's just a friend, your boss, anything but the man you love, she instructed herself. But how could she work with him and preserve her secret? If he found out, he would redouble the pressure to stay and provide him with an heir. If the pressure was of the loving kind, she might well succumb. But it would still be Amanda that he loved. It was beyond bearing, so he must never find out how she felt.

Keeping her resolution was harder than she had anticipated. Working on designs for the living-rooms, they were together frequently, whenever Lachlan could spare time from running the property.

Standing shoulder to shoulder as they pored over inventories of furniture, it was impossible not to be affected by him. A casual touch sent ripples of desire coursing through her as if it were a caress. The spicy tang of his aftershave lotion teased her nostrils. She longed to smooth the errant curl out of his eyes.

Instead, she talked of replacing modern door hardware with brass reproductions of the originals, and making templates to recast missing sections of plaster moulding. But the more they discussed hand-blocked wallpapers, the more she longed to touch and be touched by him. Keeping her mind on her work had never been more of a challenge.

It was a huge relief to discover in her diary that she was due for her monthly check-up with Dr Silvanis in Walgett. The referral had come from her family doctor in Sydney and Dr Silvanis had turned out to be a kindly, caring country doctor. She had no qualms about seeing him again.

'I'll drive you there,' Lachlan said when she broached the subject.

'No!' Her denial was so vehement that he looked startled. 'I mean, you have so much to do here.'

'You know my views on being a one-man band,' he reminded her. 'A day without my supervision won't hurt the men. Come to think of it, a day off won't hurt me either. We can collect the wallpaper you ordered from Sydney at the same time.'

She had been so preoccupied with the need to put some space between them that she'd all but forgotten the special handprinted wallpaper they had ordered for the living-room. It was a copy of an eighteen-forties design found at the home of colonial explorer, Hamilton Hume, and first reproduced for a National Trust property in Sydney.

The crimson and yellow design was in keeping with the colour schemes used in the living-room at Orana when it had been built. Luckily it was described in detail in the inventories, and Jenny had been able to discern the actual colours from paintings which showed the room as a backdrop.

Lachlan laughed, interrupting her reverie. 'You forgot all about the wallpaper, didn't you?'

Her face flushed. 'No, I ...'

He fastened keen eyes on her. 'I know what's the matter with you.'

The floor rocked under her feet. 'You do?'

'It's the baby, isn't it? They tell me that pregnancy makes a woman fuzzy-headed.'

A mixture of relief and disappointment shook her. For a moment, she feared that he had guessed her secret. 'Yes, it's probably the baby,' she said tiredly. What would she have done if he *had* guessed?

'Then it's a good thing your appointment is tomorrow,' he said firmly. 'I don't want you overdoing things.'

Walgett was the railhead for Lightning Ridge and was a good two-hour drive from Orana. The small, pastoral town stood at the junction of two major rivers, the Barwon and the Namoi. Following the Barwon River for part of the way into town, the road was scenic and green, an unusual feature in this semi-arid region of the north-western plains.

Lachlan dropped her at the corner of Fox and Wee Waa Streets, near Dr Silvanis's office. 'Would you like me to wait with you?' he asked.

Her heart leapt, until her brain tempered it with caution. Having him accompany her to her specialist was too intimate, given the way she felt about him. It conjured up images of waiting with her husband for the latest bulletin on their baby's progress. Dumbly, she shook her head then managed to find her voice. 'I'll be fine, thanks.'

'So damned independent,' he growled. 'All right, then, what about lunch?'

Intimacy was a continuing hazard. 'I don't know how long I'll be. I might do some shopping after my appointment.'

His expression became cold. 'Suit yourself.' He began to swing away from her, the set of his shoulders showing his annoyance.

Parting on such bad terms was wrong. She touched his shoulder. 'Lachlan?'

There was an odd light in his eyes as he looked back. 'Yes?'

She didn't know herself what she meant to say next because the moment was shattered by a lilting call from across the street. 'Lachlan! Jenny! What brings you two to Walgett?'

Jenny's heart sank. So Amanda was the reason why he had been so keen to drive to Walgett. He must have been hoping to run into her here. 'Hello, Amanda,' she said as the other woman joined them. From her collection of carrier-bags, she'd been shopping, although her apple-green linen skirt and jacket were better suited to a business lunch in a big city. Her supply of clothes seemed inexhaustible.

'Hi, Mandy,' Lachlan greeted her. She stood on tiptoe to plant a kiss on his cheek and his arm went automatically around her slender waist. 'How are you?'

'All the better for seeing you,' she enthused. 'Are you free for lunch?' Her question encompassed both of them but her eyes were on Lachlan alone.

His gaze swept over Jenny then back to Amanda. 'It looks as if I am. Jenny wants to go shopping after her doctor's appointment.'

'Doctor's appointment?' Amanda's eyebrows lifted.

'Just a check-up, nothing to worry about,' Jenny said quickly. For some reason she didn't want Amanda knowing about her pregnancy yet.

Amanda linked arms with Lachlan. 'Then it's just you and me.'

It always would be, if Amanda had her way. The thought made Jenny cringe inwardly but she resisted it. 'I'd better go or I'll be late,' she excused herself. Hurrying to the doctor's office, she forced herself not to look back.

The appointment went well. Dr Silvanis was pleased with her progress this far, although he chided her for being too thin. 'Usually I have to warn new mothers not to put on too much weight,' he said, wagging a finger at her.

'I eat well,' she assured him, 'especially now that the nausea has gone. But I'm also pretty active.' She didn't mention the number of times a day that she climbed up and down step-ladders, taking measurements and scrapings of paint or wallpaper. He probably wouldn't approve, any more than Lachlan did.

'You'll have to start taking things easier from now on,' the doctor suggested, as if reading her mind. 'Your ankles are a little swollen. Nothing to worry about,' he added, noting her look of alarm. 'But it would help to put your feet up more often.'

'I'll try,' she promised.

'Good.' He made some notes on her chart. 'Then I'll see you in another month.'

The waiting-room was empty when she returned to it to schedule her next appointment. The receptionist, a pleasant woman in her late teens, made a note of the date then looked with envy at Jenny's still-trim figure. 'I don't suppose we'll be seeing you in belted shirt-waisters for much longer.'

Jenny smiled. 'I was thinking the same thing myself this morning. The buttons on this dress are already under a strain.' She started to move away, then turned back. 'Where's the best place in Walgett to buy maternity clothes?'

The receptionist thought for a moment. 'A new boutique just opened around the corner in Fox Street.' She glanced ruefully down at her own full figure. 'They also sell large-size fashions. I shop there myself.'

The waiting-room door opened and the receptionist looked up. 'Mrs Farmer may know of some other good places.'

'Good places for what?' Amanda asked, coming up to them.

'To buy nice maternity clothes,' the receptionist blurted out before Jenny could intervene.

Amanda's eyes gleamed as she looked at Jenny. 'Maternity clothes? For you?' Jenny was forced to nod.

'Well, well! This *is* a surprise. Do I offer congratulations or sympathy?'

'I want the baby very much,' Jenny stated as she saw what Amanda was getting at.

Eddies of delight danced in Amanda's eyes. 'This is wonderful! Lachlan told me which doctor you were seeing so I came up on the off chance you'd be finished and we could go for coffee. How about it?'

'What about your lunch with Lachlan?'

Amanda pouted prettily. 'He met some chamber of commerce types who shanghaied him for a business meeting, so we're both at a loose end.'

But Jenny's was of her own choosing. It was unlikely that Amanda would have sought her company if she'd had a choice. Jenny wavered—she could plead shopping to do but there would be time after lunch. Besides, she could almost hear the questions buzzing in Amanda's head. They had to be faced some time. 'Coffee sounds good,' she conceded and let Amanda lead the way.

Since it was lunchtime anyway, they ordered sandwiches and tea. When it came, Amanda leaned across the table. 'Now, tell me all about your little secret.'

'It isn't a secret,' Jenny protested. 'In any case, it will be obvious to everyone before long.'

Amanda bit her full lower lip. 'All the same, you're very brave, going through it without a man in your life. Not that I'm passing judgement,' she added hastily when Jenny frowned. 'These days, single parenthood is almost fashionable. But I couldn't do it on my own.' Her gaze clouded. 'When Steven was killed in the bushfire, I didn't know how Grant and I would cope, even though Steven left us well provided for. I couldn't have managed without Lachlan's help.'

The implication was clear. She didn't intend to manage without his help now. Jenny's mind filled with a picture of them as a family and distress flooded through her. If Grant hadn't been so set on a scientific career, everything would have been perfect for them. Lachlan could have groomed Grant as his heir while Amanda gloried in her role as mistress of Orana. They hadn't bargained on Grant's special talents.

Then along came Jenny Dean. No wonder Lachlan had seized on the idea of marrying her. He wouldn't have to give up Amanda while enjoying a second chance to have the heir he longed for. A wry smile twisted Jenny's mouth. It would be ironic if her baby turned out to be a prodigy like Grant, with no interest at all in farming.

What would Lachlan do then? If he couldn't mould the child into his image, would he replace Jenny, too? The idea pained her.

'Penny for them,' Amanda said, breaking into her thoughts.

'I was thinking about your son not turning out the way you expected,' Jenny admitted fairly truthfully.

Amanda nodded. 'I wanted Grant to love the land, but I had to accept his genius for science and let my other dreams go.'

'You could have more children one day,' Jenny suggested kindly. 'One of them might be a born farmer.'

Unexpectedly, tears glimmered in Amanda's eyes. 'No chance of that, I'm afraid. When Grant was born, something went wrong. I can't have any more.'

Sympathy welled inside Jenny. 'I'm sorry. I didn't mean to pry.'

'You didn't. How can I feel badly when I have Grant and so many other compensations in my life?'

Like Lachlan, came the unwilling thought. Did Amanda know that he wanted to marry Jenny in order to have another chance at a child who would suit his needs better than Grant did? Amanda for love, Jenny for motherhood. Was that how Lachlan meant to play it? Anguish rippled through Jenny at the very idea.

Somehow she got through the rest of the lunch, but was glad when it was time to meet Lachlan for the journey back to Orana. Amanda insisted on waiting with her and the reason became clear when Lachlan arrived.

'I'm following you back,' she said. 'That is, if my dinner invitation is still open?'

'It's the least I can do, after standing you up at lunchtime,' Lachlan agreed.

Jenny got into Lachlan's car and Amanda fell into convoy behind them.

'How did the doctor's appointment go?' he asked when they were clear of the town.

'Very well,' she said, tight-lipped. 'The doctor says I'm underweight.'

'Then I'll take personal responsibility for feeding you up,' he said.

She couldn't keep the emotion out of her voice. 'You don't have to be responsible for me. It wasn't part of our agreement.'

His palms crashed against the steering-wheel, making the car shudder. 'Damn it, I want to. You know how I feel about children, Jenny. Why won't you let me help you?'

He wanted to help the baby, not her, she told herself grimly. To him she was no more than an incubator. 'I have to stand on my own feet some time,' she reminded him.

'You don't have to, as you well know. You can have a home at Orana forever, if you choose.'

She bit her lip to stop it quivering. How tempting it was to give in and let him take care of her. In the harems of the Middle East, men habitually kept some women as concubines and others as the mothers of their children. If she had been born to a harem existence, she wouldn't think it unusual. But she hadn't. Deep inside her gnawed the hope that the man she married would, as the ceremony said, forsake all others. She couldn't marry on any other terms, and they weren't what he was offering. 'It wouldn't work,' she said dully.

'You won't even given it a chance,' he fumed. 'Am I so repugnant to you?'

'No. You're a very attractive man.'

The atmosphere in the car became electric suddenly as tension crackled between them. 'Prove it to me, Jenny. Now.'

Looking back over her shoulder, she glimpsed Amanda's car following them, haloed in dust. 'This isn't the time or the place.'

His sigh was explosive. 'Then the fault *is* with me. You're repelled by what happened to me in the Sinai.'

Her eyes blurred. 'Lachlan, you don't know what you're asking.'

'Yes, I do.' He floored the brake pedal and the car jerked to a stop on the dusty verge. At once, Amanda's car pulled in behind them. Jenny twisted nerveless fingers together as Lachlan got out and went back to Amanda. Their low voices reached her, then Amanda's car pulled out again and flashed ahead. Soon she was out of sight.

'What did you tell her?' Jenny asked, her mouth dry.

'I told her you had some problems,' he said tautly. 'And you do, don't you?'

To misunderstand was the easiest course. 'I'm not ill.'

'I didn't say you were. I can't help it if Amanda thinks you are. She's meeting us at Orana. In the meantime, you do have a problem knowing what you want.'

'I *do* know what I want, and it isn't you,' she defied him with desperate urgency.

With a decisive gesture, he unclipped her seatbelt and his own, and slid his arm along the seat behind her. 'We'll soon see about that,' he said and pulled her into his arms.

CHAPTER SEVEN

THE heat of Lachlan's gaze seared Jenny. 'Do you think I haven't noticed how you react when we're together?' he demanded. 'You try to hide it but you can't.'

'You're imagining things.' Her voice was high-pitched with tension. He mustn't know how she felt—it would ruin everything.

'Am I imagining things, Jenny?' His voice dropped to a caressing murmur. 'Am I imagining the way you tremble when I touch you?'

His fingers grazed the back of her neck. To her horror, her nipples hardened in response as they pressed against his chest. The already strained buttons of her shirt-dress snapped open. She tried to bunch the fabric together but he prised her fingers away. 'Why so modest suddenly? We have slept together, after all.'

'Not in the way you mean.' Her heart lurched painfully at the admission and frustration coloured her voice.

'I'm willing any time you are,' he persisted in the same seductive tone. 'I know you want me. Perhaps you're still afraid that the terrorists did more damage than I've told you. I promise it isn't so. I'm still very much a man, so you needn't fear that I wouldn't be able to satisfy you.'

In a vivid demonstration, his hand slid inside her shirt, seeking the warmth of her breasts. Her approaching maternity had rounded them to ripe fullness and she gasped when he cupped them in turn, massaging them to pert, expectant life. Of their own accord, her hands strayed to his shoulders. 'Say you want me, Jenny,' he demanded, gravel-voiced.

'Yes, yes, I do.' The confession was wrung from her by the force of the sensations he had aroused in her.

'Then say you'll stay with me.'

The blood pounded in her ears like the surf at high tide. 'I can't,' she denied. 'Being taken care of isn't enough.'

'Then the problem *is* that I can't give you children.' He withdrew his hand and carefully closed the buttons of her shirt. As his fingers grazed her skin she flinched as if burned. He was right, she did want him. His lovemaking left her feeling molten with desire. He could have taken her here in the car and she wouldn't have possessed the will to stop him. If only he had said he loved her, instead of reminding her that the baby was his first concern.

'You don't understand,' she said into the silence which followed his return to his side of the car.

Hostility emanated from him. 'What don't I understand? That you can't trust yourself to someone you see as half a man? What's hard to understand about it? You're probably right.'

'The way I feel has nothing to do with what happened to you in the Middle East,' she insisted, but her words fell on deaf ears.

His mouth hardened and a muscle worked in his jaw. 'Your reaction tells me otherwise.'

What was the use? If she told him she loved him, he would increase the pressure on her to stay and let him adopt her child as his own. She had no alternative but to let him think he had failed her as a man. After she left, Amanda would soon restore his masculine pride. Despair flooded through her at the prospect.

Rapidly, she reached another decision. She was playing with fire staying at Orana any longer. The sesquicentenary was less than a month away. Once the restoration work was finished, she would have a legitimate reason to leave. The thought of turning up on her father's and Linda's doorstep was bleak, but at least they wouldn't turn her away.

She was so lost in her thoughts that she hardly noticed when Lachlan started the car again. The drive back to Orana which had seemed endless this morning flew past, and she got a shock when she saw that they were turning on to the gravelled driveway.

Amanda's car was parked outside the homestead. When they drove up, she hurried out, her face wreathed in concern. 'Are you feeling better now? You look a bit white.'

'It was probably the long drive,' she assured Amanda. 'I'll be all right after a rest. You two go ahead and have dinner without me.'

Amanda looked dismayed. 'We can't—I've planned it as a special occasion. Mrs Napier has pulled out all the stops.'

What was special about tonight? Too drained to discuss it, Jenny nodded tiredly. 'I'll see how I feel in a while.'

Amanda's chatter and Lachlan's answering laughter mocked her as she retired to her room. Despite pleading tiredness, she didn't feel like lying down. Her skin prickled with evocations of Lachlan's touch, and her breasts felt heavy and pendulous, craving his caress.

Thinking of how she had almost betrayed herself, her breath caught in her throat. If he hadn't insisted on blaming himself, her resistance wouldn't have fooled him for long. It was typical of the man to assume he was the reason she refused to stay. He was the centre of his universe; he wanted a child, therefore she should provide it in return for the security he was offering.

Was he so self-centred that he couldn't see beyond his imagined flaw to her needs? She didn't care whether he could father children or not—he had many other qualities she valued. But it didn't work both ways and she had to face it. He wasn't going to change.

Too restless to sleep, she decided to join the others for dinner after all. With a month to go before she could leave Orana, she would have to face them sooner or later. Nothing would be gained by hiding in her room. As well, she had her baby to consider. The doctor had impressed on her the importance of good nutrition.

'Feeling better?' Amanda asked when she joined them in the family-room. This sunny room was furnished with white cane furniture and pretty floral wallpaper. It served as a living- and dining-room while work continued on the other rooms.

'Yes, thank you.' She smiled wanly as Lachlan put a drink into her hand. It was mineral water with a twist of lemon, she noted idly. She studied him surreptitiously. He seemed relaxed, as if the scene in the car had never occurred. Obviously it hadn't affected him as much as it had Jenny. Her insides lurched as she watched him talking to Amanda. He was so near, and yet as far away as if an ocean stretched between them. It didn't prevent his Lorelei message making her want to risk the treacherous depths to reach him.

Mrs Napier's call to dinner interrupted her fantastic thoughts. She welcomed the diversion, needing it as an anchor against her errant imagination.

Following Lachlan and Amanda to the table, she was surprised to find it gleaming with silver cutlery and heirloom china. 'What's the occasion?' she asked, glancing from one to the other.

Lachlan shrugged. 'Ask Amanda. It's her idea.'

But Amanda refused to explain as she fussily settled Jenny at the head of the table, with Lachlan on her right and Amanda herself on the left. She kept up a stream of idle chatter all through the first course of chilled avocado soup, refusing to be drawn until the main course of grilled perch had been eaten.

By the time Mrs Napier had served the fruit course, Jenny was impatient with the whole performance and debated whether to plead a headache so she could escape. Then Mrs Napier placed a bottle of champagne in a silver wine-cooler at Lachlan's elbow. He opened it with a flourish and filled all their glasses. 'Now maybe we'll find out what this is all about.'

Amanda picked up her glass. 'I asked Mrs Napier to prepare this dinner to celebrate some exciting news.'

'You're getting married,' Lachlan speculated drily.

She looked annoyed. 'You know perfectly well I'm not.'

He would be the first to know, Jenny thought unhappily. She resisted the temptation to tell Amanda to get on with it.

Amanda wouldn't be hurried. 'A historic occasion marks more than the passing of the years. It also marks the passing of a torch down through the generations,' she said dramatically. 'Today I discovered that our sesquicentenary will be marked by a new arrival in the valley—Jenny's child.' She lifted her champagne glass in a toast, her face flushed with triumph.

She thought Lachlan didn't know about the baby! The realisation flashed through Jenny's mind like a lightning bolt. Was this elaborate performance meant to discredit Jenny in front of Lachlan?

If so, Amanda was disappointed. 'I'm glad you think it's cause for a celebration,' he said mildly, showing none of the shock which Amanda apparently anticipated. 'As it happens, so do I.' He lifted his glass and stood up in a smooth motion. 'To Jenny's child. A happy and healthy life.'

Confusion darkened Amanda's eyes but she managed to drink some of the champagne. 'I thought it would be a surprise,' she said, setting her glass down.

'It was a surprise, to both of us,' he said, confusing Jenny as much as Amanda.

Some of the colour fled from Amanda's face. 'What do you mean?'

Jenny's heart felt as if it were being squeezed in a vice. 'Go on, Lachlan,' she said, amazed to sound so normal, given the turmoil raging inside her. What was he up to?

'Well, who do you think is the father?' he asked, amusement in his face and voice.

Amanda wasn't the only one to look stunned— Jenny knew she looked equally stricken. Amanda stumbled to her feet. 'I didn't think...didn't know. Jenny didn't say anything.' She pushed her chair back. 'You must excuse me. It's late and I should be getting home.'

Moments later, car tyres screeched on gravel as she swung the car around and off down the driveway. Jenny waited until the engine noise died away before she turned to Lachlan. 'How could you do such a thing?'

'Do what?' His expression was bland and innocent.

'You deliberately let Amanda think you're the father of my child. If you think you can blackmail me into staying this way, it won't work.' She clasped her hands protectively over her stomach, feeling icy inside.

'It isn't blackmail,' he said calmly. 'I did it for two reasons. One, Amanda is a chronic gossip. Left to her, your situation would be all over the valley in days and I couldn't have people pointing fingers at you when they know only half the story. And two, it has ended, once and for all, Amanda's fantasy that I will marry her one day.'

'But she loves you,' Jenny ground out. How could he be so callous, using her to make his point? Was he totally insensitive to Amanda's feelings?

'She doesn't love me,' he said shortly. 'She loves having a man to lean on. I've told her over and over that she's wasting her time with me, but as long as she thinks I'm available, she keeps hoping. I like Amanda and I'm her friend, but she isn't the woman for me.'

'Because Grant didn't want the life you planned for him?'

He frowned. 'What does Grant have to do with this?'

'He's the reason you haven't married Amanda, isn't he? If Grant had chosen the land instead of science, you wouldn't have had to bother with me.'

He met her anger with maddening good humour. 'Oh, I think I may have done.'

'Don't humour me!' She noticed he hadn't argued but had deflected her accusation with a joke. Couldn't he see how transparent he was? Wearily, Jenny pushed her glass away. 'I've had enough. I'm going to bed.'

His sympathetic smile almost broke her. 'I understand. I'll have Mrs Napier bring you some milk later on.' His hand descended on her shoulder, burning through her clothes. 'Try not to worry too much. In the morning, you'll see I've done the best thing.'

The best for whom? she agonised later in the sanctuary of her room. Maybe he thought he had done what was right, but she couldn't accept it. Once word of her condition spread she would still be the butt of gossip. It would be of a different kind, that was all. And what would he tell people when she left, taking what they believed to be his child?

She covered her mouth with her hand. Was he planning to keep the baby, whether she stayed or not? The thought of fighting him in a court for custody of her own child struck terror into her heart, but it had to be considered. If by chance the child shared Lachlan's blood-type, he would have a strong case against her. Her only defence would be to prove him biologically incapable of fathering a child. Was he hoping she'd give up before it came to that?

She sifted and resifted the possibilities and the night dragged on. By morning she knew she would have no choice but to leave Orana and throw herself on the mercy of her father and stepmother.

In spite of everything, she slept late next morning. The family room was deserted and Mrs Napier informed Jenny that Lachlan was out on the property; he wouldn't be back until lunchtime. Assuring the housekeeper that the toast and fruit juice she'd set out for breakfast were all Jenny required, she took a seat at the table, thankful for the time to herself.

When Mrs Napier returned to the kitchen, Jenny lifted the phone on to the table and dialled the Sydney code and her father's telephone number. He would be at work, but Linda answered on the second ring.

Jenny took a deep breath. 'How are you, Linda? It's me, Jenny.'

Her stepmother's warm reaction took her aback. 'How lovely to hear from you, dear. The boys love your cards from the opal fields and Barry reads me your letters. You sound as if you're having a wonderful time.'

What had prompted the change of heart? 'I had some problems about the true ownership of the mine,' Jenny said tentatively, wondering how to broach the subject of her pregnancy. 'It turns out Uncle Lou didn't own the cabin after all.'

Instantly, Linda was all motherly concern. 'You poor child! So that's why you took the decorating job on that property.'

Jenny was glad that she'd explained some of her problems in her letters, paving the way for the whole story. 'I was lucky with the job,' she agreed. 'But...'

'It's more of a challenge than you expected?' Linda second-guessed her. 'I can imagine. But you're so good at this restoration stuff. I'm sure it will work brilliantly. Maybe you'll get more work in the district when they see the job you do at Orana.'

'I don't think so,' Jenny denied. 'In fact, I was thinking of coming home for a while. You see——'

Before she could complete the sentence, Linda rushed in. 'Home? Oh, no, dear. I was just this very minute writing to tell you our news.'

A cold hand gripped Jenny's heart and squeezed it relentlessly. 'What news, Linda? Tell me.'

'Well, it may not sound as exciting over the phone—I was going to send you brochures and all. Your father and I are selling this house and going off around the world together.' The joy in Linda's voice vibrated down the telephone.

It found no echo in Jenny's heart as she absorbed the fact that the home she'd known since she was born would no longer be there. Her father had dreamed of seeing the world, but they could never afford holidays, far less overseas travel. 'Has Dad won the lottery or something?' she asked weakly.

'No, it's me, silly. This dotty old aunt of mine died and left me a share in her house. It's a gloomy old place full of what I thought was junk furniture, which turned out to be valuable antiques. Imagine, Jenny! Barry and I have enough money to do the trip in style.'

'But what about Cal and Chris?'

Linda chuckled. 'They're coming with us. I've never seen two teenagers so excited. I'm not sure if it's the trip or the prospect of a year away from school, but they can't wait to get going. There's enough money to keep us for a year and we plan to invest the money from the sale of this house, for when we get back. Isn't it all too wonderful?'

'Wonderful,' Jenny echoed, feeling dizzy and sick. She had made the classic mistake of assuming that she could follow her own star while her parents kept the home fires burning for her. They had stars of their own to follow. But selling her childhood home and setting off around the world for a year was almost too much to take in.

'Are you still there?' Linda asked when the silence lengthened. 'I know it's a surprise, but Barry and I decided if we don't go now, we never will. You are happy for us, aren't you?' There was an edge of anxiety in her voice.

Jenny fought her panic. 'Of course I am,' she said decisively. 'You and Dad deserve every happiness. I hope you have a sensational year and send me heaps of postcards.'

There was a pause during which Linda's breathing grew heavier, as if she was trying not to cry. Finally, she said, 'You're a good kid, Jenny. I admit I was worried when I married your father. It seemed like my first marriage all over again. But you're different. You want us to be happy, don't you?'

'Of course I do. I'm glad my father found you.' Her praise was unstinting.

She could almost hear Linda preening down the line. 'Thanks, Jenny. It means a lot to have your approval. But I'm babbling on here. Did you have a special reason for calling?'

In a split second, Jenny knew she had two choices. She could tell Linda the truth and burden them with worry over her. If they didn't decide to cancel their dream trip, their enjoyment would be impaired. Or she could give them her silence as a gift. 'I only wanted to see how you all were,' she said, keeping a tight rein on her runaway emotions. 'Let me know how your plans work out.'

'Of course. Your employer's number was in your last letter so we'll call you before we leave Australia. I hope you'll come and see us off.'

'You never know.' It was a promise she couldn't keep without revealing her pregnancy. It would have to wait until they returned—by then her life should be in order again. It would be soon enough to have to face everyone. But it meant she wouldn't see her father and brothers for more than a year. With a heavy heart, she said goodbye and hung up.

She was glad that Lachlan was out working. She couldn't face him right now. She had been so sure that she would be on her way home to Sydney by day's end that at first she couldn't think beyond that option. But she had no choice.

After last night, she couldn't stay in the valley, although pride demanded that she finish the job she had started at Orana. The opal fields no longer provided a refuge. So what was left?

Amanda's admiring comment about her decorating skills had planted the seed of an idea. Could she teach what she knew to other women? Her own studies had been completed by correspondence. She could devise a course and advertise it, allowing students to work at their own pace to suit their circumstances, as she had done. Working people and those with small children could undertake the course, and she would be able to work right through her pregnancy and afterwards.

A glimmer of anticipation began to lighten her despair. She could survive on her own and she would!

She stared down at her hands. Survival was one thing, but what about happiness? Supporting herself while being both mother and father to her child wouldn't leave much scope for a personal life. A foretaste of the loneliness which her plan entailed swept over her. Could she survive life without Lachlan?

As always, work was her panacea. She was supervising the hanging of the handmade wallpaper in the living-room when she heard a car pull up outside. It was too early to expect Lachlan and she knew the sound of his four-wheel-drive vehicle by heart.

Moments later, Amanda breezed into the room. As usual, she looked immaculate in a lemon crêpe de Chine trouser suit with a cheeky white fedora perched on her blonde hair. She swept the hat off as she came in. 'Hi, Jenny. Mrs Napier told me I'd find you in here.' Her dark-eyed gaze encompassed the work in progress. 'This looks marvellous. You wouldn't know it was the same room.'

'It's coming together slowly,' Jenny agreed warily. Was this the same Amanda who had stormed off in a state of shock last night?

'The plaster mouldings look so authentic you'd never know they were reproductions,' Amanda commented. 'And I barely recognise the cedar panelling now you've had all that dark varnish stripped away.'

Jenny's eyes flickered upwards. 'The Victorian chandelier is my favourite discovery. It was on Lachlan's 1840 inventory but it couldn't be found, and there was no record of its disposal. We tracked it down in the attic and had it professionally cleaned. It used to belong to a maharaja.'

Amanda duly admired the chandelier and said that, yes, it was magnificent. The tension in the room grew to fever pitch. But Amanda hadn't come to discuss the progress of the work, so why was she here?

When she could stand the suspense no longer, Jenny wiped the wallpaper paste off her hands and threw the cloth down. 'Smoko-time,' she said to the workmen. At once they downed tools and rummaged in their gear for the sandwiches and flasks of coffee they brought with them. They filed outside for their break and Jenny turned to Amanda. 'Would you like to join me for a tea break?'

Amanda's pleasant expression slipped long enough for Jenny to glimpse satisfaction on her face. Then the mask was back in place. 'I'd love to join you,' Amanda agreed.

In the family-room, Mrs Napier had set out a pot of lemon tea and home-made biscuits and cake. Jenny helped herself to a slice of sponge cake which had won Mrs Napier prizes at local shows, she'd been told. Normally it melted in Jenny's mouth, but this morning it tasted like breadcrumbs as apprehension made her throat arid. She washed it

down with tea, schooling herself to be patient until
Amanda revealed whatever was on her mind.

It seemed like forever before she spoke. 'I want
to apologise for the way I behaved last night,
rushing off so rudely.'

Jenny's eyes went round. An apology was the
last thing she had expected. 'There's no need to
apologise,' she said, keeping the surprise out of her
voice. 'Lachlan had no right to say what he did,
either.'

Tears brimmed in Amanda's eyes but she gulped
them back and sipped her tea. 'No, he shouldn't.
It was an awful shock. He knows how I feel about
him.'

Compassion for the other woman welled inside
Jenny, catching her off guard. 'You love him, don't
you?' she asked gently.

Amanda nodded. 'I know I shouldn't be so de-
pendent on a man. Lachlan's always telling me so,
but it's the way I was brought up. It was always
Lachlan with me, ever since we were children.'

'Yet you married Steven Farmer,' Jenny couldn't
help pointing out.

The other woman's gaze became tragic. 'Only
because Lachlan went off to join the Air Force. I
wanted to wait for him, but he vetoed it. He wasn't
sure if he would ever come back. He knew I needed
to be married, to have a man to lean on. It's crazy
in this day and age, but it's the way I am.' She
pushed a lock of blonde hair back from her eyes
with a nervous gesture. 'I don't know how I would
have survived Steven's death without Lachlan's
support.'

Yet it was probably Amanda's dependence which kept Lachlan from loving her, Jenny saw with a flash of insight. His dislike of being what he called a one-man band on the property could extend to relationships, she saw now. There was no way he would want a woman clinging to him, expecting him to think for her.

Her thoughts were interrupted when Amanda gave a reedy laugh. 'I don't know why I'm telling you all this. I only came to discuss the progressive dinner with you.'

Having made her position clear, Amanda was now ready to change the subject, Jenny realised, caught off guard for a moment. She gave the other woman a blank look. 'Progressive dinner?'

'Didn't Lachlan tell you? It's a fund-raiser for the local children's home. Once Orana is finished, we'll invite everyone in the valley to a dinner, serving one course at each of three properties. As the focal point of the celebrations, Orana gets the dessert course with dancing here afterwards.'

'It sounds fun,' Jenny observed, unsettled by the switch from emotion-charged discussion to planning a fund-raising dinner. 'What can I do to help?'

'You're doing it with your restoration work. Naturally everyone pitches in to help with the dinner, but your main job is to make Orana look spectacular.'

'It doesn't need help for that. Wait till you see the reception-rooms once the paper-hangers are finished.'

'I'm looking forward to it.' Amanda angled her body forward. 'What will you do when it's finished, Jenny?'

The tension level rose again as Jenny sensed a trap in the question. 'I don't know,' she murmured. 'Surely it's up to Lachlan?' Amanda still thought the baby was his so Jenny took refuge in the falsehood.

The pleasantness vanished from Amanda's expression as if wiped from a slate. Her eyes were cold as she faced Jenny. The gloves were finally off. 'On the contrary, Jenny. It's entirely up to you.'

CHAPTER EIGHT

THE room kaleidoscoped around Jenny as she tried to focus on Amanda. Her cup rattled in its saucer and she put it down. If Amanda thought that the baby was Lachlan's, wouldn't any decision be his as well? 'I don't know what you mean,' she said, looking away.

'You have it all, don't you? Your career, your looks, now a baby. You can't have Lachlan, too. It isn't fair.'

The little-girl tones didn't deceive Jenny. When she looked back there was steel in Amanda's pearl-black eyes. She kept her tones even. 'Life isn't fair, Amanda. We have to make the best of it.'

The other woman tossed her silky hair in a dismissive gesture. 'You'd know, wouldn't you? The mix-up with the mine, insinuating yourself here, was all part of your plan, wasn't it?'

Jenny was even more at a loss. 'What plan?'

'This scheme of yours to snare Lachlan as a father for your baby,' Amanda supplied, adding, 'You may as well know I don't intend to lose him a second time. You see, I know what you're up to.'

The cold triumph in Amanda's expression struck fear into Jenny's heart. What had Lachlan done to this woman with his stupid, senseless innuendo? He couldn't have foreseen this outcome. Jenny shivered. 'I don't have any plan,' she denied. 'Why don't you say what's on your mind?'

Derision and sympathy mingled in Amanda's gaze. 'Very well, I will. I don't know what sort of story you told Lachlan or how you managed to convince him, but I know he can't be the father of your baby, no matter what he believes.'

An arctic sensation gripped Jenny and she clasped her hands together so hard that her knuckles whitened. 'What makes you so sure?'

With calm deliberation, Amanda spaced out her words. 'I know because when he was serving in the Middle East his squadron was attacked by terrorists, who used a chemical weapon which destroyed his ability to be a father.'

The matter-of-fact delivery didn't soften the impact of her words one bit. Each one attacked Jenny like a physical blow. Amanda knew the truth! Lachlan had asked Jenny to keep his secret but, somehow, Amanda had discovered it. How many more people knew? 'How did you find out?' she asked in a hoarse whisper.

'His ex-wife, Christine, was my friend. We got drunk together one day and she told me the whole sad story.' Her laugh was bitter. 'Don't worry, it hasn't gone any further—yet.'

Her implied threat wasn't lost on Jenny. 'You wouldn't tell anyone else, would you? Lachlan doesn't deserve that. I'm the one standing in your way.'

Amanda's eyes narrowed. 'I'm well aware of it. And you're the one who can guarantee my silence.

All you have to do is leave the valley as soon as your job here is done.'

She already knew the answer but had to ask, 'If I don't agree?'

'Then everyone in the valley will know Lachlan's secret and it will be your doing.'

The words barely had time to sink in before Jenny became aware of a movement at the door. The colour drained from her face as she looked up to see Lachlan standing there. Hot and dusty, and in his work clothes, he was still the dearest sight she could wish for. But his eyes were wintry. How much of the conversation had he overheard?

She started to her feet, holding her hands out to him. 'Lachlan!'

He dashed her hands away. 'I suppose you're satisfied now?'

Sharing his pain, she was baffled to find herself the target of his fury. 'Why should I be satisfied?'

He jerked his head towards his neighbour. 'Now you've blabbed the whole story to Amanda, you've got your own back for last night, haven't you?'

So this was how it felt to be shot. First there was the searing impact which knocked the breath out of her body, followed by the agonising pain of a mortal wound. Lachlan might as well have fired a bullet at her—his words carried as much impact. Blindly, she shook her head. 'You're wrong, Lachlan. I didn't——'

'Then it's a coincidence that I find you two discussing my sex life and Amanda saying it will be all over the valley, thanks to you?'

So he had arrived in time to hear Amanda's threat, misunderstanding it completely. Silently, she implored Amanda to set him straight, since he wouldn't believe Jenny. But the gleam of satisfaction in the other woman's eyes shattered her hopes. In despair, she pushed past him into the corridor.

He grabbed her shoulder. 'Where are you going?'

'To pack. You've made your feelings quite clear.'

His hand slid from her shoulder, leaving a trail of heat all the way down. Even now, her body betrayed her by responding of its own accord. Was she to have no peace where he was concerned? Dizzily, she turned away.

'Jenny!' His command shocked her into freezing where she was. She didn't turn around.

'Let her go, Lachlan. Don't you think she's done enough damage?' Amanda intervened.

Without waiting for his reply, Jenny fled to her room. Blinded by tears, she began to fling clothes and possessions into her suitcase with scant regard for them. If he thought she would betray his confidence and was willing to condemn her without a fair hearing, she didn't want to stay any longer. Where she was going, she didn't know, but it would be far away from Orana and its autocratic owner.

The hammering on her door startled her. She kept packing, ignoring it. The door rattled again. 'Jenny, open this door. I want to talk to you.'

Thank goodness she'd remembered to lock it. 'Go away. You've said enough,' she mumbled, her voice husky with tears.

'Are you crying?'

She shook her head then remembered that he couldn't see her. 'Of course not. I haven't done anything to cry about.'

The door vibrated again as he pounded on it. With each blow, she jumped as if he had struck her physically. 'Open this door. Please.'

The sudden plea almost made her weaken. Then she hardened her heart. He was probably regretting his hasty action because it put her baby forever beyond his reach. She had no illusions that he regretted the hurt he had inflicted on her.

'I mean it Jenny. Open up or I'll break the damned door down.'

Of course! Brute force was something he *did* understand. 'Go away,' she pleaded again.

There were no more warnings. With a crash of splintering timber, the door exploded inwards as the lock was wrenched from its mooring. The door swung at a drunken angle from shattered hinges as Lachlan thrust past it into the room.

Something snapped inside her. 'You brute!' she screamed. 'Look what you've done to that lovely old door, just because you didn't get your own way. You're a vandal, do you hear? A vandal!' She flew at him, fists flailing, and rained blows of frustration and despair against his chest.

She might as well have pounded a rock surface. He let her attack him then grasped her wrists in a grip of iron, raising her arms so she was held clear of him.

'Let me go,' she ordered through clenched teeth.

He gave a wry smile. 'Or you'll do what? Hit me? As you can see, I'm terrified.'

'I can see you enjoy showing how strong you are,' she railed at him. 'Well, you've already attacked me verbally so you may as well go the whole way.'

He held her straining wrists high in the air. 'Don't tempt me, Jenny, or, so help me, I'll make you eat those words. And I won't need to hurt you to do it.'

'What . . . what do you mean?'

'This.' Releasing her wrists, he pulled her arms down to her sides and enveloped her in a hug which kept them there. The breath was driven from her body as he lowered his head, his mouth a heat-seeking missile.

Flames of passion whipped through her as he covered her face with hot, urgent kisses. Resistance became capitulation and he felt the change in her instantly. His hands slid up, roving over her back and entwining in her hair, while he kissed her as if he would never stop. Her mouth had been a hard line of defence but, when his teeth grazed her lower lip, she gave a tortured cry and shaped her mouth to his.

Her anger fled, burnt out by the exultation of being in his arms. This was where she belonged, where her flesh throbbed in response to his touch. How could she dream of leaving?

It's not real, a small voice insisted. He knew the effect he had on her and he was using it to get his own way. He still thought she'd betrayed his secret to Amanda. His mistake lay in accusing her. He must have known as soon as he'd done it, and now he was trying to win her over again.

She finally summoned the strength to push him away, and he looked at her with passion-drugged eyes. 'What's the matter?'

She dragged stiff fingers through her tangled hair. 'This. Us. Everything.'

'I thought——'

'You thought you could make amends for your hasty accusations by making love to me. It nearly worked.' Oh, lord, how nearly it had worked.

He gestured helplessly. 'But not nearly enough.'

She turned imploring eyes to him. 'Sex for its own sake will never be enough for me.' Her long lashes curtained her pain-filled eyes. 'Is it because I let myself get pregnant that you think I don't deserve your respect? Well, I do.'

Bleakness invaded his expression. 'Hell, Jenny, don't think such a thing! I respect you as I've done few other women in my life. You must believe me.'

Her arms dropped to her sides as all the fight went out of her. 'You wouldn't believe me when I asked you to.'

'But I do believe you.' He slid on to the edge of her bed, planted his feet apart and rested his forearms on his knees. 'Hell, I'm not making much of a job of this. I didn't come in here to kiss you— I just don't seem to be able to stop myself.'

Any more than she could around him. 'Why did you come?' she asked hoarsely.

'To say I'm sorry.'

Her mouth dropped open. 'To say what?'

'Almost as soon as I said it, I knew you would never tell Amanda what happened to me. I'm sorry I thought it even for a minute.'

'It was Christine,' she said dully. 'She told Amanda about it in a drunken moment together. Nobody else knows.'

'It's some consolation, I suppose.' He studied his hands, which were ridged with red dust from the property. She longed to clasp them and wipe away those stains which reminded her of blood. 'I should have known it was Christine,' he said heavily. 'She had no more idea of loyalty than a Hereford does.'

'I'm glad you know it wasn't me. I would never do such an awful thing.' At least she wasn't leaving under a cloud. With jerky movements, she returned to the suitcase lying open on the bed.

He looked at it and back to her. 'Don't go, Jenny. I need you here.'

What she would have given to hear those words said with love! Her limbs felt heavy and uncooperative. She tried to put a few more things into the case then gave up the battle. 'I'll stay to finish the restoration,' she conceded. It was madness, but leaving was beyond her power for the moment. Why did Lachlan have to kiss her just when she had summoned the will to go?

'Thank you,' he said in a heartfelt way. 'I'll have a man come and fix your door this afternoon.'

'What will you do about Amanda?' she asked.

He sighed. 'I can't do anything except hope she has the decency to keep what she knows to herself.'

But would she? Jenny didn't share his confidence. He hadn't seen the fire in Amanda's eyes when she'd made her threat. Her silence was conditional on Jenny's leaving when her job was done, she remembered. His secret was safe at least until then.

He stood up. 'I'd like to make up for this morning. Will you let me?'

Her mouth felt bruised and her body ached from his last attempt. She shook her head. 'You don't have to.'

He cupped her chin, tilting her head so she was forced to meet his eyes. The gentleness in them made her want to cry again. 'I want to make it up to you,' he persisted. 'You haven't had much time off since you got here. I'd like to show you around Orana.'

The prospect of an afternoon in his company attracted and repelled her with equal force. Dared she trust herself alone with him? She had already seen how vulnerable she was around him—he could bend her to his will like a reed in the wind. Maybe it was her pregnancy which made her so pliable lately. Surely he couldn't mesmerise her so effortlessly otherwise?

Since her will seemed to have deserted her, she wasn't surprised to hear herself agreeing to go with him. She tried to tell herself that such moments would be precious once she left Orana. Each one would be a jewelled memory, to be relived when they were apart. Storing them up made sense. At least that was her excuse.

By the time she had changed into jeans and a long-sleeved shirt with the sleeves rolled to the elbows, Amanda had gone and Lachlan was waiting beside his four-wheel-drive vehicle.

He had changed into a fresh shirt, but his jeans and boots were still streaked with red dust from his morning's work. His crumpled bush-hat sat far back on his head, giving him a rakish, devil-may-care look. His tanned forearms were linked across his chest. Not long ago she had been inside that charmed circle. The thought sent a wave of warmth spiralling through her. Her steps faltered. She must be mad to spend an afternoon with him—certifiably crazy.

Sensing her hesitation, he closed the distance between them. 'Ready?'

'This is much too selfish of me. You must have work to do,' she dissembled.

He grimaced. 'Since sun-up I've been at the stockyard, sorting fifteen hundred head of cattle, most of which have never seen a human before. Turn your head for a second and you're dead.' Her gasp punctuated his statement. 'I think I'm entitled to some time off, don't you?'

'I never thought of running a property as dangerous,' she observed, held in thrall by a vision of his being thrown into a fence or off a horse because of a wild bull.

'It's my life.' He shrugged off the danger. 'Mustering is the best part. Riding out on horseback for a week, camping out and bringing in thousands of head of stock with the help of helicopters. It beats anything the city has to offer.

He settled her in the passenger seat and slid in behind the wheel. 'What would you like to see first?'

Distracted by his nearness, which was emphasised by the horse-man mix of scents which teased at her, she shook her head. 'I haven't seen much beyond the homestead, so it's all new.'

Taking her at her word, he took her on a guided tour of the property, stopping first at a ridge which overlooked most of the valley. From there, he pointed out the mix of black-soil plains and ridge country which comprised Orana.

As well as merino sheep, the station carried Hereford cattle and an experimental flock of angora goats. The river which bordered Orana on one side was stocked with golden perch, catfish and enormous murray cod.

From this height, the paddocks had a mown appearance and the majestic blue gums seemed to touch the sky. Mobs of doe-eyed kangaroos lay on their sides, their long legs and tails stretched out, as they sheltered from the heat of the day under trees and rocky outcrops.

Occasionally, Lachlan forgot how little she knew about farming and his talk was peppered with references to phosphate bounties, sheep dips and crop-dusting, which she barely understood. At those moments, she amused herself by watching his face, seeing how his eyes gleamed as he talked. His attachment to the land was almost tangible.

'How could you bear to leave Orana?' she asked, thinking of his Air Force experience.

His chin came up. 'It was either leave or beat the stuffing out of my father. We were like two bulls in the same paddock, locking horns over everything. It wasn't until his heart attack forced him to slow down that I felt free to come back. I'll never leave again.'

Abruptly, he swung around and headed back to the car. She followed slowly, her emotions stirred by the depths of his love for the land. What must it be like to have such a sense of belonging? Her own roots stretched no further back than her father's house, and even that was being sold. Both her parents had come to Australia from England before Jenny was born. All her relatives were English, just names to her, except for Uncle Lou, her mother's oldest brother. Her mother had followed him to Australia, leaving the rest of his family behind. Jenny had never thought of it as a loss until now.

'Where are we going next?' she asked. 'Back to the homestead?'

The road claimed his full attention until they reached the foot of the steep hill, then he glanced at her. 'We're heading towards Tillaron. I want to show you something special.'

The road circled around the homestead where some of the men were trimming grass and sapling trees along the broad swathe known as the home paddock. 'What a pity they're cutting all the greenery down!' she exclaimed. 'The house would look much prettier with a few trees around it.'

His impatient sigh whistled between them. 'It would also be potentially lethal. The open ground is there for a purpose, as a firebreak.'

Why hadn't she thought of it? During her school holidays at Lightning Ridge, she had heard the miners talk about the terrible bushfires which ravaged the area from time to time. Amanda's husband had been killed in one, she recalled soberly.

'It's just as well you aren't in the middle of a drought. It must be really dangerous then.'

'Strangely enough, it isn't. In drought conditions, the grass dies back and there's nothing to burn. It's when we have a few good seasons of rain and the grass grows really long, followed by a dry spell, that I worry.'

One glance around showed that the grass was lush and green, waving in the dry breeze. 'Is that why they're cutting a firebreak?'

'Exactly.' His hand strayed from the steering-wheel to her thigh, then he returned his gaze to the corrugated dirt road. 'Don't worry. The men know what to do if there's a fire. Everyone in the valley pitches in. You're quite safe, so don't look so anxious.'

How could she feel anxious around him? The soothing tone was one he might have used to gentle a nervous animal, and his touch was hardly intimate, but her pulses picked up speed with infuriating promptness. She was like a barometer, her body gauging her response to him with worrying precision. The trouble was, she had no idea how to stop it from happening.

They were almost at the boundary between Orana and Tillaron when, without warning, he plunged the car off the road and down a steep, jungle-clad embankment. She gave a yelp of dismay and shut her eyes. Had he gone mad?

His laughter echoed through the car as they came to a shuddering stop and he switched the engine off. 'You can look now. We're here.'

Cautiously, she eased her eyes open and drew a breath of amazement. Behind the car was a corridor of ploughed grass where they had forced a track down from the road. It ended at a billabong of such spellbinding beauty that she stared at it, speechless.

'Lovely, isn't it?' he said into her silence.

Words were inadequate. 'It's gorgeous.' Not even a breeze ruffled the emerald surface of the water. Sunlight filtered through the thick stands of eucalyptus and shoulder-high grass bordering the pool. The air was sweet with the perfume of wattle in bloom, all the more surprising for the lateness of the season. None of the wattle she knew lasted this far into spring.

He laughed at her confusion. 'I know how you feel. I felt the same way when I found this place. I was about ten years old at the time. I used to go skinny-dipping here. See, there's my rope, still hanging from that blue gum.'

Placing his arm around her shoulder, he turned her slightly. She spotted the remnant of a rope knotted around a branch which extended out over the water. She could see him clearly, his lithe brown body taut with effort and his legs gathered under him as he swung Tarzan-fashion across the pool, to drop like a stone into the water. 'This place is every boy's dream,' she murmured.

'It was mine. I owned it. It never dried up, even during the worst droughts, although its boundaries shrank quite a bit. I think it must be fed from an underground stream but I never found it, although I dived often enough to look for it.'

While he unloaded the car, she wandered along a shaded path which was just visible at the water's edge. When she returned Lachlan was setting out a picnic in a patch of shade. 'Hungry?' he asked when she rejoined him.

A feast of crusty bread, salad in a plastic container and golden chicken had appeared on plates at her feet. She curled up beside him. 'I wasn't, but I am now.'

They ate in companionable silence, washing the food down with some of Mrs Napier's home-made lemonade. 'This is sinful,' she said, polishing off the last of her chicken.

His gaze warmed her. 'Does pleasure always have to be a sin?'

She rolled over on to her stomach and propped her head on her arms. 'I didn't say it was. It just feels as if it should be.'

He grunted dismissively. 'Typical female comment.'

'Who are you calling a typical female?' she objected, made bold by the food and the surroundings. 'I'll have you know I decided my future this morning.'

Tension crept into his face. 'What did you decide?'

'I'm going to start a correspondence course for people interested in restoring old houses,' she stated, finding that she wanted his approval. 'What do you think?'

He slid down and rested his back against a tree trunk. 'It sounds like a good idea. I could have used it when I started restoring Orana, instead of having to learn by trial and error.'

'Exactly. I can tell my students how to establish what a room or a building once looked like, and how to recreate it using original or reproduced materials.'

'You've thought it right through, haven't you?' he asked.

'You don't sound very enthusiastic,' she pointed out, disturbed by the coolness in his voice.

Unexpectedly, he crushed a paper cup in his fist. 'Damn it, you know why I'm not enthusiastic. I don't want you to leave here. If you meant to start your course here, it would be different.'

The muscles in her stomach knotted painfully and she sat up. 'Does it matter where I operate from?'

'You know the answer as well as I do.' He lifted anguished eyes to her. 'Why don't you give it some thought?'

It was an effort to speak around the lump in her throat. 'Do you really want me to?'

'Of course I do, Jenny. It's all I've ever wanted since we met.'

'Oh, Lachlan.' It was just as well she was sitting down because her knees felt weak. They wouldn't hold her if she attempted to stand. 'I don't know what to say.'

'Then say yes.' His urgent demand made her want to weep. He really did want her to stay with him. He gestured around them. 'Look at this. Was there ever a more beautiful place in which to bring up a child?'

Oh, lord, they were back to the baby again. She swallowed her disappointment. 'Would you still want me to stay if I weren't pregnant?' she demanded.

His look became bleak. 'What are you saying? That there isn't a baby? It was all a lie?'

Rage bubbled up inside her and she scrambled to her feet. They supported her very well after all. 'No, it wasn't a lie. But not all pregnancies turn out the way they're supposed to.' Terrifying though it was, every new mother had to accept that sometimes things went wrong. She couldn't guarantee him what he wanted, even if she stayed.

His face went white and he towered over her in righteous fury. 'Christine said something similar before she went out and killed her child. Is that what you've got in mind?'

Quailing before his rage, she flung her head from side to side. It was plain to see that every ounce of his concern centred on her baby. 'I would never hurt my child,' she vowed, horror at the very idea trembling in her voice. 'But not because you threaten me. It's my body and my life. I can do what I damned well like.'

As she swung away from him, motivated by a desperate need to get away, he caught her and held her, ignoring her flailing limbs. How dared he suggest that she was like Christine? She could kill him for saying it. She could...

She could do nothing except tremble in his grasp as she realised that, once again, she was his willing captive. She wasn't going anywhere while he held her to him with such throbbing emotion, all his rage vaporising in a firestorm of passion which ignited the moment he touched her. Where was it going to end?

CHAPTER NINE

'LOVE me, Lachlan, please.' Was Jenny actually making such an outrageous request? She must be, because he responded by easing her on to the rug and cradling her head on his arm. His eyes were as warm as a caress.

'Why do our fights always end like this?' he murmured.

His arm, so hard and muscular when he was working, was miraculously yielding as she snuggled into the crook of his elbow. 'Were we fighting?' It was hard to remember.

His head shaded her face as he leaned over her. 'I think I was. I'm sorry for saying you're like Christine. You aren't in the least. You're much more compassionate and a lot more beautiful.' He lingered on the word and her breathing quickened. 'You also have a heart.'

'I could never hurt this baby, no matter what,' she vowed. 'You have to believe me.'

'I do.' He frowned in self-condemnation. 'I never really doubted it. Around you, I keep saying things I don't mean.'

Things like wanting her to stay? Fresh doubts shafted through her. What was she thinking of, inviting him to love her when it wasn't on his agenda? It might be in the physical sense, but love didn't begin and end in bed. Their priorities were too different.

She stirred uneasily beneath him and he rested his free hand on her thigh, his eyes dark with unmistakable desire. 'In spite of the fireworks, I could love you very easily,' he admitted.

She already did love him, to her cost. 'Because I could give you an instant family?' she probed.

His hand drifted over her rounded stomach, which gently strained her jeans. The light touch sent volts of sensation pulsating through her. More than anything, she wanted to clasp her arms around his neck and draw his tantalising mouth within kissing distance. But she schooled herself to wait for his answer. 'I must admit, it does make you a bargain. Two for the price of one,' he teased.

Her long lashes shuttered her misty eyes. 'I think this is where we came in.' She tried to sound jocular, but the reality was too depressing and her voice came out thin with pain.

He brushed the hair away from her forehead, his feather-light touch making her open her eyes. 'You seem to think I wouldn't want you to stay if not for the baby.' She noticed that he didn't say she was wrong. He took a slow, deep breath. 'The baby has nothing to do with the way I feel right now.'

While she struggled to frame a reply, his hand strayed to the buttons of her shirt. They parted to his touch and he pushed aside her lacy bra so he could stroke her breasts. The intimate touch made her senses run riot. Her sensible reply became a moan of pleasure. As he continued to explore her body with dizzying skill, her blood-pressure soared.

Wanting him became a sensation like hunger. She had never been held like this, caressed like this, *desired* like this before. The lonely places inside her ached to be filled as only he could.

'Lachlan!' She gasped his name as a wave of euphoria engulfed her. Logic flew skyward with the waterbirds taking off from the billabong. All that remained was a raw, pulsating need for his love.

'I know, my love, I know.'

With economical movements, he shed his clothes, then he began to undress her with such gentle precision that she wanted to cry. He was peeling her like an onion, revealing layers of herself she normally hid from sight. The innocent, the career person, the mother-to-be, were all discarded with her clothing, leaving only Eve, as tempted as she was tempting in their modern-day Eden.

His gentle expertise took her breath away—this was loving such as she'd never experienced. Dreamed of, perhaps, but never imagined that she could be carried on such wings of physical perfection. Lachlan wanted to give her as much pleasure as he took for himself. Each touch lingered exquisitely as he explored every inch of her until he knew her to the depths of her being. Time lost its meaning as she surrendered to sensation.

Molten with desire, she followed her instincts, charting his teak-hard body with newly sensitised fingertips. His firm muscles rippled under her hands, betraying his heightened responses.

Rolling her over again, he covered her mouth with urgent kisses, his tongue a flickering flame of delicious torment. When she thought she could stand it no longer, he lifted his head and searched her face. 'Will you let me love you, Jenny?'

Her quick nod was all the assent she could manage. Her throat was much too tight for speech, and words tangled in her mind. Finally all thoughts fled and she opened her arms, incandescent with her need of him.

He came to her with mind-shattering gentleness, his eyes never leaving her face. When she tried to draw him deeper, she saw the worry etched there. 'I don't want to hurt you,' he insisted.

Even now! The thought surfaced through her ecstasy. Even now, he was putting the baby ahead of everything else. She blinked away the mist which clouded her eyes—he was only being considerate. She was the fool. 'It's all right,' she said in a throaty whisper.

Despite her assurance, caution tempered his actions. He moved slowly, carefully, but somehow the tide carried her along, building and building until she cried aloud, arching against him to bring him closer, deeper, until their souls touched.

The wanting seemed to last forever. When it finally came, the moment of release carried her on wings of fire, to the brink of sanity, then ebbed slowly until all that remained was a marvellous feeling of contentment.

Not talking, they lay side by side in the dappled shade, enjoying the bush sounds and the delicious warmth baking into their bones. Jenny nestled into the crook of Lachlan's arm, loving the feel of his steely body against her. What was it about opposites attracting? They certainly did.

Lachlan's fingers trailed down the curve of her hip, eliciting a tremor of response deep inside her. 'Why did we wait so long?'

A V of anxiety etched her forehead. 'Perhaps we should be asking why we didn't wait longer still.'

'Because of the baby?'

'To be sure of how we feel.'

He frowned down at her. 'I'm sure. Aren't you?'

She mustn't make the classic female mistake of confusing a man's lovemaking with commitment. He wanted her—what they had shared was proof enough. And he wanted the baby. But none of it meant that he returned her love. Frustration gnawed at her—falling in love shouldn't be one-sided. It was so unfair.

Derisive laughter welled in her throat. She was being as childish as Amanda, expecting life to be fair. Why couldn't she accept what was and make the best of it? 'I'm sure,' she said heavily.

'Then marry me and stay here forever.'

Again she was plagued by indecision and the wish for things to be different. If she said yes, they could love like this for eternity. So what if it *was* one-sided—he would be a model husband and father. As a lover, he was peerless. And she loved him. It was more than many women gained from a marriage. In time, he might come to love her as well as the baby. 'Yes,' she decided in an instant.

His eyes glittered. 'Yes, you'll marry me?'

'Yes, I will marry you.' How strange it sounded said out loud! If only she had his love to set the seal on it. She pushed the thought away. She loved him and would use everything in her power to awaken its twin feeling in him. In the meantime, there was no point wishing for the moon.

His magnificent body was taut with excitement. 'Heaven be praised! I've known that we belonged together since the day I first saw you at Lightning Ridge.'

Some of his joy transmitted itself to her and she smiled mischievously. 'Even though I turned your invitation down?'

'You were splendid. Free-spirited, sure of what you wanted, in charge of your own life.'

She rested her linked hands on her sun-toasted stomach. 'Which just goes to show how little you knew about me. None of those impressions was accurate.'

His languid smile warmed her. 'The reality only made me more sure that you were the woman for me.'

The baby was an important part of that discovery, she felt sure. Chilled suddenly, she sat up. When he had his heir, would Lachlan have any love left for her? Or would it be out with the old, on with the new? In with Linda, out with Jenny. Or Derek's 'hello, I must be going'.

'You're thinking again,' Lachlan accused her. 'I don't like the worry I can see in your eyes.'

'I'm not worrying,' she denied. 'I was just...oh, my!' Her eyes went round as saucers as she registered a faint but definite fluttery sensation in the depths of her womb. A broad grin of recognition spilled on to her face.

'What is it?'

'My baby just moved. Dr Silvanis said it would happen some time soon. I just felt it for the first time. My baby moved!'

His warm hand slid across the pit of her stomach, provoking fresh flutters which had nothing to do with her pregnancy. '*Our* baby,' he said decisively. 'From now on we're in this together.'

He wasn't wasting any time laying claim to her child, she thought with a pang. In his mind, they were already a threesome. It would take her longer to accept the idea. 'Our baby,' she repeated experimentally.

His jaw muscles worked. 'Lord, it's true. I'm finally going to be a father.'

'I thought you didn't want to be responsible for other people?'

'This is different.' He thought for a moment. 'Why don't we announce our engagement at Amanda's progressive dinner? It will be a historic occasion in more ways than one.'

He sounded like the cat with the cream, she thought ruefully. He was looking forward to fatherhood before he was even a husband. But she had agreed to marry him, knowing what his priorities were. She had no one to blame but herself. If only it didn't hurt quite so much.

It wasn't until they were in the car, on the way back to Orana, that Jenny remembered Amanda's threat. Lachlan's lovemaking and proposal of marriage had driven it from her mind. Appalled, she tore her gaze from the road to Lachlan. Should she tell him? He could try to convince Amanda that she would gain nothing from spreading cruel gossip. It wouldn't win him back for her.

Without a man in her life, Amanda needed Lachlan's support. They had been friends since childhood. Jenny didn't want to destroy their friendship if it could be salvaged. She decided to say nothing for now and talk to Amanda herself before the engagement was announced.

As it turned out, it was touch and go whether the progressive dinner took place at all. By the time the day came, the valley was plagued by dry thunderstorms which set everyone's nerves on edge, as much due to the electric charge in the air as to their very real fears.

'Prime bushfire conditions,' Lachlan said worriedly as they drove to Tillaron, where the main course was to be held.

'We could turn back. I shan't mind,' she assured him yet again. Now that the time had come to face Amanda, she didn't relish the confrontation.

'If I don't turn up, the others will stay away too,' he maintained. A few of the local farmers had already missed the first course at Priscilla Downs. Lachlan's presence had reassured the others. 'Amanda has worked hard over this dinner and the children's home is depending on it. We can't drop out now and disappoint any of them.'

Amanda would be much more disappointed by the time it was over, Jenny accepted soberly. She wondered if he knew it.

'The men know how to handle a bushfire,' he added distractedly, as if to reassure himself as much as Jenny. 'And all the buildings are equipped with lightning conductors.'

Although he minimised it, his concern sent up worry-flares inside her. 'Do they know where to reach you if... if anything happens?'

'Of course.' He braced his arms against the steering-wheel then relaxed them. 'Let's stop worrying and have a good time.'

Although she tried to take his advice, Jenny felt taut with nerves. The stormy atmosphere only added to her anxiety. It was an effort to be pleasant to the sixty or so guests gathered at Amanda's home for the next stage of the fund-raising dinner.

Some of them, Jenny knew from local church gatherings. Others were strangers to her. One day she would know them all, as Lachlan's bride.

Lachlan's bride. How eerie it sounded, although she'd had almost three weeks to get used to it. The baby kicked regularly now and seemed to take a perverse delight in waking her during the night. 'Our baby', Lachlan called it delightedly. He played the part of expectant father with such enthusiasm that she wondered how he would have coped if the child had been biologically his. He would have been impossible! If she was honest, her role as mother of his child meant more to him than his bride.

She summoned a smile as Amanda approached carrying an enormous tray of hors-d'oeuvre. When she saw Amanda's savage expression, the smile faded quickly. 'What have you done?' she demanded, then lowered her voice. 'Lachlan just informed me that he's going to announce your engagement tonight.' Her fury was so intense that the food jumped on the tray, and she put it down. 'I warned you what would happen if you insisted on staying.'

'Even if I leave, it doesn't mean he'll marry you,' Jenny said more calmly than she felt. Amanda had worked herself up to the verge of hysteria. 'Don't you think he would have proposed to you already if he was going to?'

'Thanks to you, I'll never know what he would have done, will I?'

Aware of the curious looks they were attracting, Jenny tried to draw her into an alcove, but it was like trying to shift a statue. 'I want us to be friends,' she said. 'I can't make Lachlan love you.'

Amanda's eyes blazed with unreasoning fury. 'Maybe not. But I can make him hate *you*. When I'm through, everyone will know he couldn't have fathered your child. How long do you think your love will last then?'

Jenny's heart was a tight, hard ball in her chest. She couldn't let this happen to Lachlan. His pain was her agony, too. There was one last hope. 'If Lachlan tells you himself that he won't marry you, will you accept it as the truth?'

A luminous look lit Amanda's face. 'He would never say anything so cruel. He knows how I feel.'

'Then let him drive you back to Orana for the dancing. The two of you can talk on the way.'

Suspicion clouded Amanda's raisin-dark eyes. 'Where will you be?'

'I'll take Lachlan's car and drive back on my own.' She touched the other woman's arm urgently. 'But please, don't say anything to anyone until you've spoken with him. Please?'

Amanda's chin lifted defiantly. 'I won't have to. By the time we get to Orana, Lachlan will be mine. You'll see. He won't choose a baby over me.'

Amanda's uncanny perception rocked Jenny to her core. So she wasn't the only one who recognised how much Lachlan wanted to be a father. Poor Amanda. If Grant had been more interested in life on the land, Lachlan might have married Amanda long before Jenny came on the scene. No wonder she resented Jenny for usurping what she saw as her place.

The rest of the dinner passed with agonising slowness. The seating arrangements kept Jenny and Lachlan apart and, although she made an effort to converse with her dinner partners, her heart wasn't in it.

The food was outstanding but it might as well have been cardboard for all the pleasure she took in it. The first course of pea and lettuce soup washed down with a fragrant chablis had been served at Priscilla Downs. Now they were served crown roasts of lamb raised on Tillaron, the roast stuffed with apricots and brandied prunes. A robust burgundy complemented it perfectly.

Normally, Jenny would have enjoyed the sumptuous meal. This was her first progressive dinner and the experience intrigued her. But tonight her tangled thoughts gave her little peace. What if Lachlan couldn't make Amanda see reason?

When she'd decided to go through with her pregnancy alone, Jenny had steeled herself to cope with the inevitable gossip. But to have everyone know about Lachlan's plight was too much. Every time they went out together as a family, it would be like flying a flag. The baby isn't his. He can't give her any more.

'Are you all right, dear?'

Forgetting her surroundings, she had allowed a trickle of tears to escape. 'I'm fine.' She smiled for the benefit of the kindly Presbyterian minister on her right. He was a dear man and she had been thinking of asking him to christen her baby. 'Some food went down the wrong way,' she added to allay his concern.

He patted her hand in acknowledgement and launched into a monologue about vegetable growing which she gathered was his hobby. Thankfully all she had to do was nod and look interested.

A lemon sorbet was served as a palate cleanser. Soon it would be time to move on to Orana for the dessert and cheese courses. As her contribution, Mrs Napier had prepared *tulipes* of thin, crisp biscuit filled with honeydew melon ice-cream and green grapes. Local cheeses and fruit from Orana's orchards would complete the meal.

Across the vast table, Jenny saw Amanda talking to two other women. One of them, she vaguely recognised. Then it came to her. She was the doctor's receptionist who had advised Jenny on where to buy maternity clothes.

Their eyes met and the younger woman waved. Jenny lifted her hand in acknowledgement then turned to the man on her left, a retired shearer who lived in Walgett. All the time she was talking to him, she was aware of glances flickering back and forth between Amanda's group and herself. What was Amanda telling them? Surely she wouldn't make good her threat before she had talked to Lachlan?

Breathing became a chore suddenly, and the stormy air felt empty of life-giving oxygen. Jenny felt light-headed. She would have to speak to Lachlan as soon as the course was over. He should know what Amanda had in mind. But before she could seek him out, he came around to her side of the table. 'Will you be all right on your own for a while?'

'Where are you going?' Panic threaded her voice.

'To look at Bob's new utility,' he explained. 'It's parked out the back. I'm interested in buying one and he's offered to let me take it for a test run.'

What a time to look at a car, she thought, feeling slightly hysterical. Before she could stop him, he had drifted outside with a group of the men. They would probably share a few beers and a smoke before they rejoined the ladies. Peculiarly Australian etiquette it might be, but it was the way things were done in the bush.

She looked around at the rapidly emptying table. An inspection of Amanda's collection of paintings by local artists was to follow this part of the dinner. At the end of the evening, one of the works would be raffled to boost the fund-raising effort. Most of the guests headed for the room which had been turned into a gallery for the day.

'Coming to look at the paintings?' the minister asked her, touching her arm. Since her momentary lapse at the table, he had fussed over her with fatherly concern.

She shook her head, making the decision even as she spoke. 'I have to get back to Orana to help Mrs Napier with the next course.'

Surprise registered on his lined face. 'You can't mean to go by yourself?'

'Why not?'

'If the storm breaks, you could be caught in it.'

Was that all? 'Don't worry, I'll be all right,' she assured him and broke free to go in search of her hostess.

Amanda was supervising an army of helpers in the kitchen when Jenny burst in. 'I'm going now,' she announced.

'Going? Where?' Amanda had sampled more of the wine than was good for her. She giggled. 'Oh, yes, back to Orana.' Her smile died abruptly. 'But you mustn't. Lachlan said——'

'Lachlan can drive you back in your car, as we agreed,' Jenny asserted. She prayed that he could make Amanda see sense, although the other woman's giggly state made her doubt it.

'Tell Lachlan I'll see him at Orana,' she said. She let herself out through the front door.

Like the other drivers, Lachlan had left his keys in the ignition. Luckily he had chosen to drive the Commodore instead of his four-wheel-drive monster. Jenny slid into the front seat. There was nothing here she couldn't handle.

The dinner had started early so she would be driving most of the way to Orana in daylight. The road was clear enough in her mind, but driving in the dark was another challenge altogether.

She needed all her concentration to manage the strange car on unfamiliar roads, and it was some time before she relaxed enough to take note of her surroundings. Her relief at being away from Tillaron was tempered by worry at the metallic greyness of the sky. Hardly a leaf stirred in the still air. At the side of the road, a kangaroo sat erect, its ears twitching as if sensing danger. The heaviness in the air frightened her.

In the eerie stillness, not a bird moved in the trees. The thigh-high grass looked brittle, the green turning to silver for want of rain. She put her foot down, fighting the corrugations in the road, and prayed that the storm wouldn't break until she reached the homestead.

Her wish was only partly granted. She was well inside Orana boundaries when the storm hit with terrifying suddenness.

The stillness was shattered by a whooping, screaming wind which swept down on to the car and tore at the brittle trees, throwing dead branches into the air like giant playthings. Great streaks of blue-fire lightning ripped the sky apart then plunged to earth to spear the paddocks with shards of lethal light. Thunder pounded at her slender body, blasting through the hands she clamped over her tortured ears.

There was no point in trying to drive. The smashed trunks of silver wattle and eucalypt were hurled all over the road. A branch ploughed through the windscreen, showering her with fragments of safety glass. She huddled into the seat as the wind found her. Only her seatbelt saved her from its howling clutches.

Now she understood why the minister hadn't wanted her to set off alone. He must have known what was coming. In her innocence, she hadn't known enough to be afraid.

Again and again, lightning tore across the sky and the thunderous crashes came so closely together that there was no time to brace herself from one to the next. She screwed her eyes shut and prayed for it to be over.

In the paddock on her right stood the skeleton of a giant blue gum, its white, dead limbs arching upwards in supplication. As if answering its prayers, the heavens cast down a lightning bolt of breathtaking fury and beauty, painting the trunk with deadly blue-purple light. The light scribbled up and down the trunk then the whole tree exploded and tongues of flame surged into the sky, showering the tinder-dry grass with electric sparks.

Once started, the fire spread at breakneck speed, licking up grass, trees and fence posts until flames ran in sheets across the paddock. Finding its voice, the fire roared as released gases fed the flames. The road was the least obstacle in its path.

The heat finally roused Jenny to action. She had to escape or be incinerated in the car. But where could she go? Ahead and behind were tunnels of fire.

'It never dried up.'

As if he were with her, Jenny heard Lachlan's voice. The billabong! It was near the road to

Tillaron. It must be on her left somewhere. If she reached it, she might live through this nightmare.

A tartan rug lay on the back seat. She hugged it around herself and crouched low, pushing her way out of the car.

Radiant heat from the road seeped through the soles of her shoes and she hurried in the one direction the fire had not yet cut off. There was no sign of the billabong. Frantically, she scanned the horizon as the fire's hot breath inched closer. If she didn't reach the water soon, it would all be over.

Smoke-blind, she almost missed the faint trail of crushed grass where Lachlan had made a path down from the road three weeks ago. It had nearly grown over but was still discernible. Weeping with relief, she plunged into the thigh-high grass, slipping and sliding in her haste to reach the water.

Ahead of the flames, the wildlife was fleeing. Black cockatoos screeched overhead, fraying the black smoke with their wings. Wombats, kangaroos and possums bounded ahead of her through the grass. Intent on survival, they paid her no heed.

The water was ahead of her, she could sense it. Then she broke through, plunging into sticky mud as she misjudged its closeness. Without stopping, she tore her feet out of her shoes and plunged into the green shallows, towing the rug with her. So far the wind had kept the fire moving away from the billabong. She prayed it wasn't heading for any of the homesteads.

Sheltering against an overhanging bank, she saturated the rug and draped it around her shoulders. Lachlan must know about the fire by now—one of his men would have seen the smoke and given the alarm. Please, let it be soon. If the wind changed, the fire would race down upon her and she had no idea whether or not she would be safe in the water.

The smoke clawed at her throat, threatening to choke her. She pulled a corner of the soaked rug over her mouth and drew a lungful of air that was robbed of its heat. If she continued to breathe through the rug, at least she wouldn't choke to death.

There were many other ways to die in a fire, she thought with a feeling of distraction. It was as if she weren't really there at all, just her body crouching in a waterhole, shrouded in a wet blanket, waiting for the fire to engulf her.

Above her head was the grassy hollow where Lachlan had made love to her. Was it only three weeks ago? She had never dreamed that her Eden would change so utterly into a deadly inferno.

They might not find her until it was too late, she thought with the same terrible detachment. Lachlan would think she was at Orana, and they would assume she was still safely at Tillaron. The thought didn't shake her icy feeling of remoteness. What finally breached her detachment and brought sobs of despair tearing from her throat was realising that it could be the end for her baby, too, before it even had chance to live.

She dived beneath the sodden blanket, breathing through it as erratic gusts of wind poured waves of heat over her. The air smelt of eucalypt gas and smoke. On the bank above her, spiders of flame ran up the tree trunks and a blast of heat reached her like the breath from a furnace. She knew what it meant—the wind had changed. The fire was coming this way.

CHAPTER TEN

THERE was nowhere to run, nowhere to hide. 'Lachlan, Lachlan,' Jenny crooned, speech hurting her smoke-seared throat. She would die here and her baby too. She would never see him again.

Dark smoke billowed across the sky, the clouds laced with veins of red where flames fed on the eucalyptus gases escaping from the burning trees. One of the burning fragments landed on her blanket, sizzling as it went out. She brushed the cinder off as if it were a loathsome spider. A dead tree branch fell in front of her, its stump smoking. A column of ants used it as a bridge, crawling out across the water as far as they could go then clustering at the tip, their antennae waving.

She knew how they felt. She was out on a limb, too. Why hadn't she listened to the minister when he'd told her not to set off alone? Would anyone think to look for her here, in the heart of the inferno? If they did, how could anyone reach her through this searing, choking nightmare scene?

She screamed as a dark shape crashed down on top of her and the water reared up in steaming waves. She recoiled, thinking a kangaroo had taken refuge in the billabong. In panic, she beat at it, trying to push it away.

Unbelievably, strong arms clamped around her, quelling her panic. 'It's all right, I've got you. It's all right.'

'Lachlan? Oh, my goodness, it *is* you!' Through the smoke, the sight of his black-streaked face was like a miracle. 'How did you find me?'

'I was test-driving Bob's ute when I saw the smoke. Bob carried a radio so I alerted Tillaron and Orana. When I saw the burned-out car up on the road, I thought...hell, I still can't believe you're safe.'

Nothing could harm her. Her heart sang and she pressed close to him, pulling the wet rug around them both. 'The fire was all around me before I knew it, then I remembered this place.'

'Thank goodness you did. But what the hell were you doing out on the road by yourself? Didn't Amanda tell you to wait until I was ready to drive you back?'

So that was what Amanda had been about to say. What had possessed her to let Jenny take such a risk? The answer was here beside her. Love did crazy, dangerous, insane things to everyone. Try as she might, she couldn't blame Amanda for anything. 'It was my fault,' she said. 'I wouldn't listen to her. I wanted to go back.'

'But why? You knew I was going to announce our engagement after dinner.' He fixed her with a penetrating glare. 'You haven't changed your mind?'

With the world disintegrating around them, there was little point in pretence. They could die here tonight, but first he would know how she felt. 'I hadn't changed my mind. If anything, I'm surer than ever. I love you, Lachlan Frost.'

She was shouting above the roar of the fire, which screamed like a train in a railway tunnel. Through the streaks of smoke and soot, Lachlan looked stunned. 'You what?'

'I said I love you, Lachlan Frost. I have since the moment we met and I will until death us do part.' Even this thought couldn't dampen her elation at finally being able to confess her feelings. This was no time to dissemble.

He threw his head back and laughed. 'You crazy, wonderful woman. You sure pick your times!'

Her stomach muscles cramped in protest. He hadn't said he loved her in return. Well, what did she expect? She knew why he wanted to marry her. It was enough that he knew she loved him.

When he took her in his arms, the sense of homecoming was almost more than she could bear. Through her wet clothes, her breasts strained proud and ready for him, and he cupped them with hot-eyed fervour, crushing her to him as if he would never let her go.

She wanted him with every fibre of her being, knowing that it could be the last time they would share anything in this life. The fire was not yet upon them, but it leapt inside her at his touch, the flames crackling along her veins like whips, cracking open any last vestiges of constraint.

'I love you,' she repeated, savouring the words as if they were gifts, as indeed they were, to him.

He crushed his mouth against hers, blotting out the awful inferno above them, carrying her on wings of joy to a private haven his mouth sculpted for them alone. In the water, his hands glided over her hips and down to her buttocks, moulding her against his lean hardness.

In feverish abandon, her hands roved over his shoulders, down his back and hips, her fingers memorising every muscle and sinew like a blind person discovering a statue. The water plastered his clothes to his magnificent body so nothing was hidden from her exploration. With her hands, she made love to every inch of him.

'Hell, Jenny. How could I live without you?' He thrust long fingers into the tendrils of damp hair clinging to her head, and pressed his lips to hers with desperate hunger. Her lips parted and the kiss became a lover's dance of flickering tongues and sensuous nips as he played a passionate duet on her mouth.

As he continued the dance down her spine, every part he caressed joined the tremulous dance in celebration of her love for him.

'Love me, for pity's sake,' she urged, driven almost out of her mind by the totality of her response to him. If they had to die, let it be in a glorious crescendo of passion, not feebly but magnificently. Fate owed them at least that much.

Lachlan tore his mouth from hers. 'The fire is almost upon us.'

She was beyond fear. 'Let it come. I'm not afraid as long as I can die in your arms.'

His slate-blue eyes studied her feverishly as if committing her face to memory for all time. 'So be it.'

The water hampered them and the wet rug over them dragged them down, but desperation lent wings to their movements. The waterhole was heating now, or was it the fire of their love boiling over into the shallows?

Heat pulsated along her limbs, whether from the flames or from his closeness as he explored every inch of her with impassioned haste, she didn't know. Abandoning the last of her fear, she wrapped herself around him, drawing him into her before the fire could cheat her of his love.

Time seemed to stand still. The roar of the fire receded, replaced by the roaring of the blood in her ears and the frantic pounding of her heart in harmony with his. She arched against him as wave after wave of mind-shattering sensation surged through her. Her hands clawed at his back and he gripped her shoulders with savage possessiveness.

Afterwards, an unearthly calm invaded her and she curled against him, pressing her face against his chest to shut out the choking smoke. She let herself go limp. There was no need to fight any more.

Pain screamed through her skull as he grabbed a handful of her wet hair and jerked her head back. 'Jenny, wake up!'

Tears slid from her eyes down her sooty cheeks. She looked up at him, not understanding. 'What is it?'

'You can't give up. I won't allow it. You must wake up and fight. Damn it, you have to live for my sake.'

He couldn't let her curl up and die because of the baby, she realised as she massaged her smarting skull. Damn him, she had bared her soul to him and this was how he repaid her. 'Don't worry, I'm not giving up yet,' she said, betrayed to the depths of her being. How could she have thought that the last few minutes would change anything?

Fearfully, she lifted the rug and surveyed the ravaged landscape. The moist leaf litter around the billabong had kept the fire at bay as it crept closer over felled trees and branches. Now and then it reached for the crowns of the trees but fell back, lacking the energy to consume the living trees. From somewhere she recalled that a crown fire was the most terrible of all, explosive in its might and fury and beyond any man's power to fight.

'Jenny?' Lachlan's voice raked her. 'You're not to drift away.'

Bitterness rose in her throat like bile. 'I'm not drifting anywhere. If we survive this, you'll have your precious child.' But never again would he have her love for the asking, she promised herself. She would *not* be used like this. No matter what it cost, she would deny herself his arms as long as he withheld his love. She was hurting herself much more than him, she recognised—Amanda would be only too willing to render aid and comfort if his wife let him down. But her pride wouldn't let her give any more than she had already done.

'There'll be a blackout in a minute,' he forecast.

The eyes she turned to him were round with apprehension. 'How do you know?'

The unyielding hardness of his expression cut her like a knife. 'Fires follow a pattern. First the flames and smoke, then the blackout as the fire passes overhead. Then, heaven willing, the worst will be over.'

If they survived to see it; she heard his unspoken fear. The idea of the fire passing over them filled her with terror. But there was nowhere to hide. The billabong offered the only sanctuary for miles.

Exploratory tongues of flame appeared through the fallen trees then the fire leapt upward and surged towards them, finally gaining a foothold on the shrubbery at the water's edge. A gigantic roar deafened them and a huge rosette of fire boiled into the air. It came from somewhere near the road. 'That was the ute going up,' Lachlan said impassively. She was amazed that it had taken so long. Or was her sense of time distorted by the madness around them?

'Here it comes,' he said, and pulled her deeper into the water. The blackout swooped over them like the closing of an eye. The darkness fuelled her panic and she clawed at the wet rug, trying to tear it off her face. Lachlan grasped her hands and clamped them at her sides until her panic subsided.

The air was on fire, the darkness suffocating. Her throat was raw and her lungs screamed for pure air. Smoke poured into every fold of the blanket.

The roar was thunderous. She was sure she screamed, but no sound penetrated the fire's bellowing voice. Heat such as she had never known engulfed her. Her skin felt as if it were melting. Only Lachlan's arms around her reminded her that she was still alive. She felt as if she were being roasted in purgatory.

It was probably no more than a few minutes before the fire passed over their hiding-place, but it felt like a lifetime. 'The worst is over now,' she heard Lachlan rasp. His hold on her slackened and he lifted the sopping rug a little to peer outside.

'Is it over?' No sound came from her parched throat. She tried again, coughing. 'Is it over yet?'

'The worst of it is. We'll have to stay here until it burns itself out, but we should be safe now.'

How truly miraculous their survival had been didn't penetrate her consciousness until she forced herself to look around the blasted landscape. The fire had passed over them, consuming all the trees and grass around the billabong and setting fire to the logs hanging over their heads. Lachlan threw water over a dead tree which still smouldered above them. It went out with a hissing sound like a sigh of regret.

Night was falling. In astonishment, she realised that they hadn't been in the billabong for much longer than an hour, although it felt like an eternity. The western sky was lit by an orange glow which could have been sunset or fire, and the ground steamed and hissed as pockets of fire burned themselves out.

'Do you think anything survived?' she asked timidly, frightened by his air of withdrawal. Where was her friend, her lover?

'I think the wind turned before the fire reached the homestead,' he said in a clipped voice. 'It doesn't matter. It's only a house. People are more important.'

'Of course.'

Isolated by her thoughts, she drew them into herself in a hard ball of misery. She couldn't believe she had been so stupid as to confess her feelings to him when she'd thought they had been about to die. It was obvious that he didn't welcome her declaration of love. People were important, but not as important as a child who could bear your name. It was all he wanted from her and he was angry because she had burdened him with more.

Her cry of torment refused to be silenced. Why hadn't he let her give up instead of willing her back to life? The sound jolted him out of his reverie. 'Jenny, what is it? Are you hurt?'

To the depths of her soul—but he meant was she burned by the fire. Her skin felt scorched and raw, and blisters were already forming on her shoulders and the back of her neck, which had borne the brunt of the heat. 'It's all right,' she said apathetically. The pain was minor compared with the agony of her spirit.

'Let me take a look.'

As unmoving as a shop dummy, she let him lift the rug gently off her and inspect her shoulders and neck. For the dinner, she had worn a sleeveless silk

camisole over narrow-legged pants of the same
filmy material. They clung to her, soaked and
muddy from the pool, offering almost no pro-
tection from the fire.

Icy water sluiced over the blisters, relieving them.
'It's the best I can do for now,' he apologised. 'Are
you hurt anywhere else?'

She held out her palms, which were blistered from
her escape from the burning car, and from beating
out the flames landing on her blanket. 'It's not too
bad, considering.'

He laved water over them, then unexpectedly
lifted her hands and kissed each palm in turn with
infinite gentleness. Tears slid down her cheeks,
making runnels through the soot blackening her
face. In some ways, his compassion was harder to
bear than his aloofness. At least if he was icy and
withdrawn she could use anger as a defence. When
he caressed her like this, she had no defences left.
'What about the baby?' he asked, his voice harsh
with the effects of the smoke.

'I'm not sure. I haven't felt any movement for a
while.' Her pulses hammered as fear gripped her.
'You don't think...?'

He grabbed her wrists, holding them so tightly
that she feared for the blood circulation. 'No! We
haven't survived this for you to lose the baby now.
I won't let it happen, do you hear?'

All would be well because he willed it, she
thought bitterly. When the fire was at its height he
had refused to let her give in. Now he was fighting
for his real prize, the child she carried.

But there were some things even Lachlan couldn't control by an act of will. Things like a miscarriage, she thought bleakly as warmth trickled down her thighs. Vicious pains stabbed her, as if hot needles were being thrust into her stomach. The ordeal had been too much. Nature was exacting its price.

Could fate be so cruel as to let her survive the fire only to take her baby away now, when the worst was over? 'I'm sorry,' she whispered to Lachlan as she pitched forward into his arms.

The snowstorm swirled all around her, blinding in its whiteness. Trying to wipe the snow away from her eyes, she was hampered by thick white mittens on her hands.

'It's all right, Miss Dean, you're quite safe.'

Someone was holding her hands, preventing her from lifting them to her face. She struggled to see through the curtain of snow.

Gradually, a man's face swam into focus. He was also clad in white, but a stethoscope dangled from his neck. She was in bed, in a hospital, and her hands were swathed in bandages. But how? Where?

She must have spoken aloud because the doctor smiled reassuringly. 'You're in hospital in Walgett. I'm Dr Corrigan. The firefighters brought you in from Orana.'

Orana. The fire! The full horror of what had happened came flooding back and she screwed her eyes shut against the memories. Then she opened them wide and struggled to sit up. 'Lachlan! He was with me. Is he all right? Where is he?'

The doctor held her upper arms and eased her back on to the pillow. Nodding to someone out of her line of sight, he stepped back and a nurse moved closer to the bed. Jenny was hardly aware of the needle sliding into her veins. She was too busy fighting back tears. Where was Lachlan? He must have known she was losing the baby and couldn't bear to be around her now she was no longer of use to him.

She slept fitfully, dreaming of being ringed by fire with Lachlan outside the flames, beyond her reach. Voices penetrated her drugged sleep. They spoke softly but snatches reached her. They wanted to tell her something but they didn't think she was strong enough yet.

When full consciousness returned, she was alone but thankfully clear-headed this time. She looked wearily around at the hospital clutter, noting without any real interest that a clear tube led from her arm to a bottle hung above the bed. None of it mattered. She knew what they were keeping from her. She had lost the baby and Lachlan as a result. The doctor she remembered from her first awakening looked in, and she braced herself for confirmation of what she already feared.

'Good, you're back with us.' His cheerfulness sounded forced as he checked the chart hanging at the foot of her bed. He made a few notes then replaced it and came around to her side. 'How are you feeling?'

'Tired, flat.'

His fingers dropped to her wrist. When he released it, he said, 'It's to be expected. You had a terrible experience. It's a miracle you survived.'

'Was there much damage to Orana?'

'The homestead is still in one piece but the fire burned a five-mile swathe across the paddocks. It's part of the cycle of life in the bush, but it's still awesome to behold.'

She inclined her head. The fire would live in her memory for the rest of her days. 'How did I get here?' she asked.

'Lachlan Frost brought you in. The firefighters wanted to take you off him but he wouldn't put you down until you were safely in the hospital's care.'

A lump the size of an egg rose in her throat. 'Lachlan *carried* me out of that terrible fire?'

'He wouldn't leave your side until he knew you were safe. We practically had to drag him off for treatment in the end.'

'Lachlan was injured? How badly? You must tell me!' She was half off the bed, ready to take the doctor by the throat and shake him until he told her the truth.

Alarmed, the doctor reached for the buzzer dangling from the bedhead. He tried to settle her against the pillows but she was too edgy to be soothed. 'Tell me what you meant!' she demanded, her voice climbing with fear for Lachlan.

A nurse burst into the room and flashed the doctor a questioning glance. He shook his head.

'It's my fault she's overwrought. I said more than I should about the man who brought her in here.'

'Then I suppose we'd better tell her the rest,' the nurse concurred. 'It should have waited until she was stronger.' There was a note of censure in the woman's voice.

Jenny stifled the scream bubbling in her throat. She didn't want any more tranquillisers distracting her from what she needed to know. 'I'm all right,' she said as levelly as she could. 'Please tell me about Mr Frost.'

The doctor and the nurse exchanged glances. 'Very well,' the doctor conceded at last, 'your friend was hurt in the fire. We didn't realise how badly until he collapsed after bringing you in here.'

Panic clawed at Jenny's throat but she fought it. 'How was he hurt?'

'Burns to his back and shoulders. He may need skin grafts, but we're hoping to avoid them.'

'But he was all right. I saw him.'

Dr Corrigan shook his head. 'It happened after you collapsed. While he was carrying you out, a burning branch fell across his shoulders. Most of the damage was done then.'

She pushed aside the covers and slid her legs to one side of the bed, gripping the edge as a wave of dizziness hit her. 'I have to see him. Take me to him.'

The doctor's mouth twisted with wry amusement. 'He's been demanding the same thing since he was admitted. But you mustn't move. I'll have him brought here, but only for a short visit. Both of you need to rest.'

After they'd gone to fetch Lachlan, Jenny realised she hadn't asked them about the baby. She already knew the worst, but it would be more real when she heard it from the doctor.

The door burst open and a wheelchair-bound figure pushed through it. 'I can take it from here,' Lachlan said over his shoulder. Shrugging, the nurse closed the door behind him and he wheeled himself up to the bed. He was clad in pyjama trousers and his magnificent torso was bare except for the dressings on his shoulders. His skin glowed red as if from a day spent in the sun.

Now that he was here, shyness engulfed Jenny. What could she say to the man who had saved her life?

They spoke at the same moment. 'Jenny, I——'
'Lachlan, I——'

Laughter dispelled some of the tension. 'You first,' he prompted.

'Thank you for everything,' she said in a husky voice. 'It's all my fault that you're hurt.'

'Nothing that won't mend,' he assured her, dismissing what must be dreadful pain. 'The same thing could have happened if I'd been with the firefighters, so you mustn't blame yourself. I'm just thankful you're alive and well.'

He had to know some time, if he hadn't already worked it out. 'I'm alive, but the baby...' She couldn't go on.

He kicked the wheelchair aside and slid on to the bed, resting a hand on the curve of her hip. 'Don't torture yourself, Jenny. You're alive and that's all that matters to me.'

She stared at him in astonishment. 'But what about the baby? You wanted it so much.'

'You talk as if it's already over. Has Dr Corrigan told you it's hopeless?'

'Not in so many words, but it must be after all that happened.' She fought the hope welling up from her core. He couldn't have meant what he just said. 'You don't mind?' she whispered in disbelief.

'Of course I mind, for both our sakes. You wanted the baby as much as I did. But as long as I have you, nothing else matters. Science is wonderful. There may be a way for us to have another some day. Or we could adopt a child. But if it never happens, it's enough that I have you.'

The world tilted crazily on its axis. 'But the baby was the reason you wanted to marry me.'

His hand grazed her chin and she shivered with pleasure. '*You* are the reason I wanted to marry you. Of course I'd love and cherish your child, because it's part of you. Sheltering in that billabong, I realised that you are the most important element in my life. You, Jenny Dean, not your offspring.' His hand worked its way under the blanket and rested on her thigh, making her feel dizzy with longing for him. Was this really happening or was she still dreaming?

'I never guessed you cared for me,' she breathed. 'I thought it was only because I could give you the child you wanted.'

'And now you know the truth, I have to know something, too. Did you mean what you said before the fire overtook us? You don't care that I can't give you more children?'

Colour rushed into her cheeks. Thinking it was all over, she had confessed her love for him and begged him to hold her until the end came. 'Yes, I meant it,' she said, ducking her head to conceal her misty gaze from him. 'All I want is for you to love me.'

He would have none of it. 'Look at me, Jenny,' he commanded. When she obeyed, there was no concealing the love which shone from her eyes. He drew a taut breath. 'For goodness' sake, how are we going to last until the wedding, confined to separate rooms in this blasted hospital?'

'There are such things as bedside ceremonies,' she said shyly, then saw that he was taking her seriously.

'By heaven, we'll do it,' he agreed. Her hands crept up to his shoulders but she jumped away when he gave a gasp of pain. 'It's all right, I'll live,' he said, dismissing his injuries.

She knew he wouldn't want her to dwell on them either. 'It isn't as bad as falling down an opal mine, is it?' she ventured daringly.

'It was the luckiest fall of my life,' he vowed. 'I'd do it again if I knew it would end like this.'

A discreet cough at the door alerted them. 'Pardon the intrusion, you two.' Dr Corrigan sounded amused. 'I have some news for Miss Dean.'

Her euphoria was swept away in a cloud of apprehension. They must have decided she was strong enough to hear the worst at last. 'Is it about the baby? It's gone, isn't it?'

The doctor unsheathed some large acetate panels which looked like negative photographs. 'Not unless the ultrasound is showing phantoms these days. They're both fine.'

It was too much to take in. Her baby was alive. The pains at the billabong had been a false alarm, brought on by her ordeal. Lachlan was watching her with a bemused expression. The reason hit her seconds later. '*Both* fine?'

'That's what I said. Do twins run in your family?'

She blinked hard. 'Why, yes. My father was a twin and I have twin brothers.'

'There you go. You're having twins, boys as far as we can tell from these.'

Lachlan slapped his thigh. 'Opal miners, what did I tell you?'

He was right again. But most wonderful of all, he had said he loved her *before* they knew they were expecting a ready-made family. There was no way she could doubt his love now. Her heart swelled with joy almost beyond enduring.

'This seems like a good moment to give you something,' Lachlan said, fishing in his pocket. 'I had Bob bring it from Orana when he came to visit this morning.'

In his palm was a small white box. Her bandaged hands were too clumsy to open it so he did it for her and held it before her astonished eyes. 'My Harlequin opal!' she exclaimed. The chequer-board pattern winked and gleamed at her from a brand-new white-gold setting.

He sobered. 'I told you it belongs to you. Maybe this time I can convince you to keep it.' He glanced down at her swathed left hand. 'That is, when you have a finger free to receive it. I christened the stone Lightning's Lady after the lady who struck my heart like a bolt of lightning.'

He placed the open box on her bedside table where she could see it with every turn of her head. 'I'll wear it always,' she promised with all her heart. 'I love you so much.'

Even Amanda's threat no longer mattered. The shock of the harm she had almost done to Jenny might be enough to silence her for good, but if it wasn't they were strong enough to deal with any gossip. Nothing could hurt them as long as they loved each other.

Neither of them heard the door close discreetly behind the doctor. Embracing with bandaged hands was a challenge, but Jenny thought she did rather well as she clasped Lachlan around his waist, careful of his injuries. His chest grazed hers, hard and warm, and the prickles of new beard teased her face.

Tears of pure joy clustered in her eyes and he kissed them away, drop by drop. When his mouth claimed hers she knew there would be no more tears—at least not of sorrow. Not as long as Lachlan loved her the way he was doing now.

HARLEQUIN
Romance®

This June, travel to Turkey with Harlequin Romance's

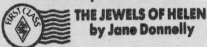

THE JEWELS OF HELEN by Jane Donnelly

She was a spoiled brat who liked her own way.

Eight years ago Max Torba thought Anni was self-centered—and that she didn't care if her demands made life impossible for those who loved her.

Now, meeting again at Max's home in Turkey, it was clear he still held the same opinion, no matter how hard she tried to make a good impression. "You haven't changed much, have you?" he said. "You still don't give a damn for the trouble you cause."

But did Max's opinion really matter? After all, Anni had no intention of adding herself to his admiring band of female followers....

RELIVE THE MEMORIES....

All the way from turn-of-the-century Ellis Island to the future of the nineties...A CENTURY OF AMERICAN ROMANCE takes you on a nostalgic journey through the twentieth century.

This May, watch for the final title of A CENTURY OF AMERICAN ROMANCE—#389 A>LOVERBOY, Judith Arnold's lighthearted look at love in 1998!

Don't miss a day of A CENTURY OF AMERICAN ROMANCE

The women...the men...the passions...the memories...

THIS JULY, HARLEQUIN OFFERS YOU THE PERFECT SUMMER READ!

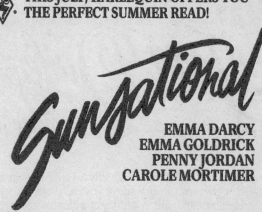

EMMA DARCY
EMMA GOLDRICK
PENNY JORDAN
CAROLE MORTIMER

From top authors of Harlequin Presents comes HARLEQUIN SUNSATIONAL, a four-stories-in-one book with 768 pages of romantic reading.

Written by such prolific Harlequin authors as Emma Darcy, Emma Goldrick, Penny Jordan and Carole Mortimer, HARLEQUIN SUNSATIONAL is the perfect summer companion to take along to the beach, cottage, on your dream destination or just for reading at home in the warm sunshine!

Don't miss this unique reading opportunity.

Available wherever Harlequin books are sold.

SUN

Back by Popular Demand

Janet Dailey
Americana

A romantic tour of America through fifty favorite Harlequin Presents® novels, each set in a different state researched by Janet and her husband, Bill. A journey of a lifetime in one cherished collection.

In June, don't miss the sultry states featured in:

Title # 9 - FLORIDA
   Southern Nights
   #10 - GEORGIA
   Night of the Cotillion

Available wherever Harlequin books are sold.